Hampshire
hants.gov.uk/library

KT-398-516

Gunman's Walk

Clint Ryker

A Black Horse Western

ROBERT HALE · LONDON

© Clint Ryker 2009
First published in Great Britain 2009

ISBN 978-0-7090-8770-0

Robert Hale Limited
Clerkenwell House
Clerkenwell Green
London EC1R 0HT

www.halebooks.com

The right of Clint Ryker to be identified as
author of this work has been asserted by him
in accordance with the Copyright, Designs and
Patents Act 1988

HAMPSHIRE COUNTY LIBRARY	
C014945789	
HJ	16-Nov-2010
AF WES	£12.99
9780709087700	

Typeset by
Derek Doyle & Associates, Shaw Heath
Printed and bound in Great Britain by
CPI Antony Rowe, Chippenham and Eastbourne

CHAPTER 1

BIG MAN, FAST GUN

Coder came into Trinity in the dark of the night, the moon a feeble slice in the sky and the stars too few to shed much light. He walked with the reins of his tired horse looped over his left arm. He passed a drunk holding a heated argument with a yellow hound over the salvage rights to a can of meat. The drunk turned and yelled something incoherent after Coder but he kept walking, his face shadowed under his hat and the yellow glow of a street lamp falling briefly across heavy shoulders.

He walked slowly now, dusty boots dragging a little in the gravel. He felt the legacy of the long miles in his legs and the small of his back.

Ahead of him the narrow street opened up into the central block. Ground lanterns and oil lamps threw yellow islands of muted light into the shadows. Two saloons remained open and the gleam of the hotel porch lamps behind a curtained window offered a silent welcome to the traveller.

There was hot food to be had in Trinity, good whiskey and a feather bed. These simple comforts tempted him but the manhunter ignored them. There were worse things than hunger or weariness when your name was Ryan Coder. Failure, for instance. He'd never been able to accept failure with any grace – also, aching back, played-out horse and empty belly notwithstanding, he was not going to tolerate it tonight while there was still a card left to play.

So the latecomer with the tireless, shambling tread turned at the next corner and headed for Luke Welker's house on Texas Street. He'd last seen the leathery old ex-outlaw ten days before when he'd passed through Trinity on the trail of killer Ned Constantine, who hailed from Trinity and was a known associate of Welker's.

The old rogue had vehemently refused to supply any information on the killer then, and although Coder still believed Constantine to be somewhere in the wilds where he'd lost his trail, he was not prepared to pass up on the chance that Welker might have heard something fresh of his quarry in the period since they'd met last.

A humourless smile touched the corners of his mouth.

Luke Welker had not been pleased to see him the

first time by daylight and in the comfort of a saloon.
So it was hardly likely the crusty old cow-thief turned
rancher would be any happier to see him in the
middle of this dark night, uninvited and unexpected.

He tethered the prad beneath a cottonwood tree
on the Texas Street corner and walked on. He kept
to the shadows until reaching the broad open space
that had once been the parade ground of the army
depot.

Before him loomed the Welker house.

Once used as officers' quarters, the large, two-
storey building had lower walls of adobe bricks
supporting a wooden frame superstructure lined by a
row of tall windows. A wide sheltered verandah ran
the full length of its front and reached down the
south and north sides.

Rustling had been good to Welker and the man
was comfortably fixed.

Coder knew he lived alone here in his big house
and also knew where he slept – in a room at the
north-east corner where a tall peppercorn tree grew.

He made no sound as he mounted the porch. A
bulky mass hanging from the gallery rafters just
around the corner turned out to be a side of beef.
Welker's bedroom door stood propped open to the
summer's night, deep snores drifting out.

The room lay in total darkness. Coder paused just
inside the door for a moment while his eyes grew
accustomed to the gloom. Dimly visible was bureau
and washstand. The snores continued uninter-
rupted. He lowered himself to a chair at the bedside

then reached out and shook the sleeper by the shoulder.

Welker came awake with a grunt and rubbed at his eyes until realizing there was someone there.

'Who the blue-eyed Judas—?'

'Coder.'

Welker swore viciously and tried to roll out of bed before steel fingers clamped on his scrawny arm.

'Simmer down, Welker.' Coder's voice was deep. 'I just need to ask a few questions.'

The oldster continued to struggle. When he failed to free his arm he lashed out with a bare foot. 'You dirty, back-shootin' polecat! I ain't talkin' to you now or—'

His words choked off in a gasp of agony as Coder twisted his arm. Hard. He made to speak again but another twist caused him to slump against his pillow, helpless with pain.

Coder let him go and jabbed a finger into his chest. 'You asked for that and got it, Welker. You ready to talk now or will I really go to work on you?'

Even men who knew the bounty hunter well weren't always sure when he was bluffing or deadly serious.

Welker was hurting enough by this to make the latter guess.

'All right . . . what the freak is it you want? And afore you start, I know nothin' about Ned, if that's who's on your mind. I ain't seen him in a month and that's the truth.'

Coder leaned back.

'What would you know about the truth, you lying old bastard? Anyway, I was patient with you last time but that's all used up now. I know he slipped into the high country since and I reckon if anyone can guess where he might be holing up, it's got to be you. So, let's cut the crap and hear what you know.'

'You got no right, Coder . . . goddamnit, you ain't even law!'

'Names!'

'You're nothin' but a—' the whiskery old reprobate began but flinched when a fist waved close to his nose. 'All right, all goddamn right! Where d'you say you lost Ned?'

'In the hill country above Fallon's Crossing.'

'Judas man, that's forty miles from Trinity. I don't know that country way out there.'

'I say you do!'

Welker sucked in a ragged breath. Again his eyes searched the hard brown face in the gloom and he shivered. He was a tough old man yet knew the other could be double hard and vicious with it when he must be. 'OK . . . Fallon's Crossin'. . . . There's a place in the Sundances about seven miles south-east of Fallon's where I used to hole up sometimes when I was – when I was working with cattle—'

'Thieving cattle,' Coder corrected. 'Where is this hideout?'

'Well, you go across Pearl River at the ford south of Murphy's Station and then you—'

Welker broke off in mid-sentence as a light footstep sounded on the porch outside. Beyond the windows, a dim shadow moved. Welker jerked erect and Coder's hand clamped his arm again.

'Who's that?' the bounty hunter hissed.

'I don't know – I swear it!'

Coder came out of his chair. Through the window he could make out the tall shape of a man standing close by the hanging side of beef. After a moment the man turned and weak moonlight gleamed briefly on fiery red hair.

Ned Constantine was red-headed!

The bounty hunter's fingers dug brutally into the flesh of Welker's upper arm as he slipped the Peacemaker from the holster.

'Don't make a sound,' he warned. 'Don't even breathe!'

When Ryan Coder entered Trinity, Ned Constantine was in the house of Kitty Dechine which stood on the east side of the Welker yard some fifty yards from the house.

The hardcase had shown up in town a bare thirty minutes earlier at the end of a punishing ride from the north-west. The killer was tired but triumphant as he kicked off his boots and threw himself upon the feather bed. He grinned as he reflected on how he'd thrown Coder off his scent days earlier, considered it had been a touch of genius to return to his home-town. Who would ever suspect he might do that? Not iron jawed Coder, he was sure. And certainly not the lawdogs who'd placed the thousand-dollar bounty on his head for shooting a woman up in Granite. All those manhunters would be out beating the brush for him right now while he rested in safety and comfort right here in Trinity.

'Kitty!' he yelled.

Kitty Dechine, a richly contoured widow of thirty-five who was only one of wild Ned's many paramours, stepped into the room from the kitchen.

'I'm powerful hungry, Kitty,' he said. 'What have you got in the larder?'

'Not much, I'm afraid, Ned. There's only a little bread and cheese. But Luke Welker slaughtered a steer this afternoon. It's hanging on the porch of his house. I can go cut you a steak. Luke won't mind, seeing it's for you.'

Kitty returned to the kitchen to get her butcher knife.

She was on her way to the front door when Constantine emerged from the bedroom.

'I'll go get the meat, Kitty.'

'No, Ned,' she protested. 'You should stay indoors. It's dangerous for you to go out.'

'Hell, it's only across at Luke's. Besides, I got nothin' to worry about here in Trinity.'

'But that big man who was here before – Coder. He scared me, Ned. He looked like a man who'd—'

'Just another blown-up rep, baby.' Constantine grinned, taking the knife. 'He'll be lucky even to find his own way home after the way I lost him.' He slipped an arm about her waist and kissed her. 'Now stop frettin', woman. I'll be back with the steak in jig time. We'll put away a good feed than get down to the serious business of makin' up for lost time.' He pinched her bottom.

'Oh, Ned!' she laughed. 'You're just not afraid of anyone, are you?'

'Nothin' in the blue-eyed world, baby,' said the man who'd shown no fear at all when he'd gunned down a helpless woman.

He slipped away into the night.

All seemed serene to the lean figure who strolled from Kitty's house. A deep hush lay over the sleeping town. The mass of Luke Welker's house loomed before him. There was no movement, no sound to suggest danger, nothing to put him on his guard. He planned to cut off a generous slab of steak. There was no better cook in Trinity than Kitty.

He was about to mount the porch when it happened. A sudden sense of danger seemed to touch him. It was a tingling that began in his legs and ran up his backbone. He propped, looking this way and that, puzzled.

Nothing stirred.

There wasn't even a breeze to disturb the leaves of the pepper tree. His eyes played over the house. Nothing. He was not a nervous man by nature, but only Ned Constantine himself knew how he'd been sweating ever since learning Coder was on his trail days earlier, for Coder was the manhunter they claimed simply never quit.

He shrugged the uneasy feeling away and inhaled deeply. Ahhh! That felt better. He was simply a little trail-worn and edgy; no need to get jittery or start staring around expecting an ox-shouldered bounty hunter to loom out of the night. Pull yourself together and think of just one thing: fresh-killed beef!

He mounted the gallery, glanced at the windows of Welker's bedroom, then reached out and ran a hand over the side of beef hanging from the ceiling rafters on a hefty hook.

The big knife glinted and he began to cut.

In his darkened room just ten feet away Luke Welker didn't seem to breathe as he watched Coder's bulk move towards the door. The man's throat constricted with tension as he turned his head stiffly to see Constantine pause in his cutting to take a fresh grip on the beef. Coder paused to stare back at him and the ancient hardcase felt the chill of fear. Coder terrified him, yet his hatred of the bounty man was even stronger. He hated with rare intensity any man who wore a badge or was even remotely involved with the workings of the law.

And suddenly he could hold back no longer. 'Ned!' he howled. 'Watch out!'

Coder's curse sounded as he went lunging headlong through the doorway. The knife dropped from Constantine's hand as he clawed for the gun on his hip. The Colt came up with incredible speed and his eyes blazed like an animal's in the deep gloom. The thunder of Coder's gun shook the building to its foundations and the bullet slammed home. The impact sent Constantine spinning off the gallery into the house yard. Yet somehow he retained his balance, and triggered. The slug whined over a crouched Coder's left shoulder. The bounty hunter fired again and Constantine whirled, took two erratic steps towards the pepper tree and fell dead.

Gunsmoke rose silently around Coder's set face as he rose slowly from his crouch. Bare feet sounded in back of him and Welker rushed out to gape in shock at the body of the outlaw who had been his protégé.

'Ned!' The oldster's voice was a shriek.

The cry brought sudden fury to Coder's face. He swung the gun and the blow caught Welker in the mouth, spinning him off the gallery to crash headlong into the yard.

'Aiding and abetting a bloody-handed butcher!' he accused, his thumb drawing back gun hammer. 'A man ought to—'

Looming over Welker Coder presented a frightening sight. But the old badman was too dazed and shocked to be scared now – just mad.

'You're just what they say you are, Coder. Nothin' but a rotten killer!'

Coder stopped then straightened. His enemies claimed he was a rock and not a man. But if he was granite then a chink appeared whenever that term 'killer' was directed his way. That was the one barb that would always sting.

Yet the moment swiftly passed and his bronzed features were expressionless by the time he holstered, went to the corpse and with ridiculous ease hefted it and slung it over one shoulder.

Staring straight ahead he appeared not to see

14

Welker rise on hands and knees before him until he suddenly kicked out to send the man rolling away gagging with pain. Coder's step didn't falter and he didn't look back as darkness claimed him and his burden.

Lights were coming on all over the town by the time he'd slung the dead killer across his horse and headed down Texas Street at a walk. Men who came running in their night shirts propped and stared, blanching when they recognized the red-headed body slung across the stallion's back.

He heard someone whisper 'Constantine!' Then another shouted, 'Lucky Ned's been killed!' – and the street hummed with hate.

Coder didn't slow his pace nor make a move for his six-gun. Not a single onlooker made a play and the bounty hunter would have been surprised if anyone had. For he knew people like this only too well. They might well make heroes of badmen here yet this rarely translated into action. At least Lucky Ned had had guts. It may well have been his only virtue.

He went directly to the telegraph office where a badly frightened operator fired his telegraph message off to Mission informing Sheriff Salem Beeber that he would be bringing Constantine in and for him to have the bounty money ready.

He 'rewarded' the operator with the responsiblity of taking charge of Ned Constantine's body until daybreak, then went back along the now-hushed street and checked into the hotel.

From his windows he watched townsfolk moving

through the gloom below, calling to one another across the night. His lip curled and he jerked down the shade before touching a vesta flame to the lamp.

The low bunk looked enticing. He stripped to the waist and treated himself to a thorough cleansing with strong lye soap, the light gleaming on his heavily muscled torso as he scrubbed.

He wiped his face dry and studied his image in the framed mirror above the washstand. No change showed, he thought. Yet violent death should leave some mark, he believed ... and told himself yet again that things must change. He was a manhunter by trade but the killing was taking its toll. Yet studying cheekbones, dark unblinking eyes and skin burned the colour of saddle leather, he knew he could easily pass for a law-abiding cattleman with his own spread, a traveller in leather goods maybe, or even pass for an outdoor kind of travelling preacher man ... most likely.

Then he sourly recalled that painted woman in Abilene who'd once remarked, 'You look like a man who's seen and done everything!'

'Leave it, Coder!' he said aloud and flung the towel aside and went to the bunk. He slung his six-gun and holster over the bedpost where they would be within easy reach, then checked the lock on the door before blowing out the lamp.

He stretched out and felt the iron tensions and fatigue immediately begin to ebb. He lay in darkness and thought about his next job, then forced his mind to blank. Soon he was alseep.

The ranchhands had to help the old man out of the buggy, but once his feet were firmly planted on the ground, he shook their hands away and leaned upon his silver-topped stick. He stared up at the lofty façade of Mission's Frontier Hotel for a time, the scorching Texas sunshine beating down on his bare head. Eventually he hunched his shoulders and shuffled slowly forward.

The handsome young woman in the green travelling suit and broad-brimmed hat came to his side. She made no attempt to help him navigate the steps, knowing that to do so would draw a sharp reproof. Passers-by paused to watch as he laboured up to the long gallery, many recalling how he'd once strode through the town like the range king he'd once been, but could never be again.

He halted before the doors to swab his sweating face with a kerchief. A tailored grey suit hung loose on a once powerful frame. Illness had robbed his face of all colour yet he was still impressive with that stubborn jaw and keen blue eyes. The girl sniffed in the direction of the hotel, then turned to confront him squarely.

'It's still not too late to change your mind, Father.'

'I never apologize and never change my mind,' he snapped. 'You should know that better than anybody.'

'Danny is dead . . . he must be.'

'I've told you never to say that.'

'He's dead and we both know it. You'll only make yourself ill and unhappy sending somebody else to search for him.'

'I'm sick and unhappy right now.'

'Father, you've wasted heaven knows how much money searching for Danny. What makes you think a man like this could succeed where others have failed?'

'The simplest reason possible. They claim he's never failed to bring back any man he's gone after.'

'He hunts live men, although mostly they are dead when he brings them back, or so I've been told.'

'Open the door.'

'Father—'

'The door!'

Libby Wardlaw sighed and did as ordered. The cattleman limped past her to enter the lobby. The shades were drawn against the glare and potted palms created an impression of coolness. The clerk glanced up from his desk and, recognizing the couple, hurried to greet them.

'Mr Wardlaw, Miss Libby,' he gushed. 'We are honoured to—'

'Where is Coder?' the old man cut in.

'I believe he's up in his room.'

'Then go tell him I'm here. Quickly, man, quickly.'

The clerk took the stairs two at a time. Libby Wardlaw touched her father's elbow and indicated a chair. But Wardlaw shook his head and remained standing until the clerk reappeared. Alone.

'Er . . . Coder will be down presently, Mr Wardlaw.'

'Presently?' Wardlaw scowled. 'My appointment was for ten and it's past that now. What's keeping him?'

The clerk just shrugged and scuttled off to his desk leaving the couple to stand in the centre of the lobby for several long minutes before finally hearing a heavy tread upon the stairs.

Coder paused with one hand on the railing. As usual he was dressed in brown and wore a gun rig buckled around his hips. He was clean-shaven and his skin was a deep bronze in the dim light. His impersonal gaze flicked from father to daughter and the girl stiffened under that hard stare.

'He looks exactly as I expected, Father!' she whispered. 'This is a mistake!'

Before Wardlaw could reply Coder started down. He crossed the floor to them and halted with a nod.

'I'm Coder.'

'Wardlaw,' the rancher replied. 'My daughter Libby. You're late, Mr Coder.'

'So?'

'I abhor tardiness. I don't care for—'

'Let's get something straight. You might be rich and carry weight around here but to me you're just another client who wants a risky job done. I'm here to take it on if it shapes up. So why don't you cut the jaw and get down to cases? The man you sent to see me says you want me to find your son.'

'How dare you speak to my father—' the girl began angrily, but Coder spoke over her.

'His name is Danny and he left here three years

ago after you quarrelled. Right?'

'I can see you are a very direct man, Coder,' the cattleman said, tight-lipped. He seemed to falter a little then sat down, the girl hovering at his side. He waved her away and straightened. 'Very well, I'll concede Danny was always wild and rebellious and we quarrelled frequently until, as you say, we parted under strained circumstances.'

'So I hear. Last night when I arrived I asked some about you folks. I know now that your son was a bit of a hellraiser and might have wound up in State Prison if his father hadn't been Justin Wardlaw. I picture your son as flashy, trigger-tempered and mostly on the edge of trouble. Does that sound like him to you folks?'

It seemed a long moment before Libby Wardlaw could drag her eyes off the manhunter. She turned to her father, who had gone pale.

'Now perhaps you'll listen to me, Father? Surely it must be obvious now just what sort of man this is you're thinking of sending after Danny?'

'He does have a hard tongue,' Wardlaw conceded, rising. 'But I also sense he has the ability to handle what can only be a difficult and perhaps risky job of work.'

He nodded at Coder.

'The doctors have given me only a short time to live, Coder. I wish to be reunited with my son before I die and am prepared to pay handsomely if you succeed in finding him and return him here. I'm convinced he's alive but probably living under an assumed name. He may not want to return but I believe a man of your reputation and ability should be able either to induce or force him to agree. Does that sound an honest enough proposition to you, sir?'

'Honest enough.'

'Then may I have your answer? Yes or no?'

'How much?'

'One thousand dollars.'

'A deal.'

CHAPTER 2

MANHUNTER

Slashing teeth ripped through his brown shirt sleeve and grazed the heavy biceps, Coder retaliated with a chop across the paint's muzzle causing the animal to to rear backwards. But a jerk of the head harness bought him down again and an iron hand clamped over the stallion's quivering right ear, causing the animal to freeze.

'Don't try that again,' he warned softly. 'Or they'll be renaming you Old One-Ear.'

The paint quivered with impotent rage but made no attempt to retaliate, leaving Coder free to complete the saddling without incident.

The conflict between horse and rider was of long standing. Coder had acquired the big paint two years earlier in the New Mexico mountains after killing its Apache owner in a knife fight over a water canteen. The horse had never forgotten or forgiven that incident and the manhunter would carry some of the scars of their ongoing feud to the grave. The stallion was vicious, pig-headed and treacherous but could run for longer than a man could sit a saddle. To someone of Coder's profession this made it valuable beyond price.

The horse had quietened down some by the time he led it out into the afternoon sunshine. It was always frisky following a spell and this showed by the way it stamped and tossed its mane that it was ready for the trail.

As was Coder.

He was feeling good about his latest assignment, knew how badly he wanted to get away from jobs that might lead to gunplay and dead men. He'd always regarded himself as a searcher and finder rather than just another hardcase with a quick gun. Sure, Danny Wardlaw sounded like a hellraiser and rebel, but often youngsters like that could be handled and tamed, if you knew how to go about it. He envisioned himself casting a wide net over the south country to snare the wild boy eventually then to convince him he was needed back home with his folks for a spell.

He grinned sardonically. *Sounds simple when you say it quick, Coder.*

He was adjusting the bedroll when the girl appeared around the corner of the livery stables. The sight of her caused him to pause a moment before continuing with his small chore.

She came to stand directly in back of him and he caught the subtle fragrance of her perfume mingling with the fresh, clean smell of her. She was waiting for him to acknowledge her presence but he didn't turn. Instead he plucked the Winchester from the saddle scabbard and began brushing the polished walnut butt with his sleeve with faked concentration.

'Mr Coder?'

He didn't turn. 'Yeah?'

'Will you kindly face me when I'm speaking?'

He flicked a speck of dust from the barrel, squinted down its gleaming length then rammed the piece back into leather. He adjusted his stirrup and patted his saddlebag, only then turning to face her with heavy shoulders straining against the seams of his dark brown shirt.

'What?' he asked. His tone was curt. He sensed she didn't like his style or reputation – maybe both.

Libby Wardlaw lifted her chin. She had a strong, determined jawline which contrasted with her mouth. Her lips were full and soft – lips such as a man might dream of during long nights on the lonesome trails when there was nothing but the wind and the stink of danger for company.

'I want to know if there is any way I can talk you out of accepting this job for my father?'

'What's the matter, missy? Don't you want your brother found?'

'My brother is dead!'

'You said that before. But your dad thinks different.'

'Danny was so wild, so full of things I could never understand. We haven't heard a word from him in years, so he must be dead!'

'Then I don't see what you've got to worry about. If he's dead I'll find that out and it'll save your father thousands of dollars searching for him in the long run. Anything else?'

She shook her head and some of the purpose appeared to drain from her face. 'No, it's not all. If . . . if Danny were alive—'

'Now, just a minute. You just said you're sure he's dead. You can't have it both ways.'

'I said I still believe he's dead!' she flared. 'But if there is one small chance he may still be alive then you are the last person I would want going after him.'

'Why?'

'Surely you must know?'

'I'm asking you.'

Her lip curled. 'Your reputation, Mr Coder – the man who brings them back . . . dead! The way you brought that Constantine outlaw in yesterday! If by some chance my brother were still alive it's almost certain he would not wish to return home voluntarily. So he would resist. And what would be the predictable outcome of that, Mr Coder? My brother draped across his saddle shot full of holes, perhaps?'

He smiled thinly. 'You don't think a lot of me, do you, missy?'

'I do not. And I will thank you to stop calling me that—' She broke off and Coder could see she was fighting for control now. She made a small gesture with a gloved hand, then continued in a quieter tone. 'I'm sorry, I didn't want to quarrel with you.'

'That a fact? I thought you did.'

'Mr Coder, I shall try to explain my feelings the best I can. My father is dying as you already know. Lately he's had far too much time to think about things and has become preoccupied with Danny. He now feels he might have been responsible for all the trouble between the two of them and wants a reunion before he dies.'

'Understandable maybe?'

'Possibly. But I'm sure whichever way this turns out it will only bring my father added misery. Should you discover that Danny was dead, then Father would grieve for him. But if by some chance he's alive then I am certain he would still defy my father, which again would be terrible for him. So, Mr Coder, I'm asking . . . no, begging you not to undertake this search.'

The man of the gun was silent a moment, studying her. Finally he said, 'I take it you love your father?'

'Of course I do.'

'And he loves your brother?'

'Yes. But—'

'Then I guess that's it.' Coder fitted foot to stirrup and swung up. 'Sorry, but I've got to turn you down.'

Tears brimmed the girl's eyes. 'But why this talk of love then? What does that have to do with it?'

'More than you might even guess, missy,' he grunted. He touched fingers to hat brim and kneed the stallion forward. '*Adios.*'

She started after him then halted, a sudden gust of wind pressing the green dress against long legs.

26

Coder glanced over his shoulder and saw her touch a lace handkerchief to her eyes.

He swung away into Main Street.

The citizens of Mission were out in force to watch him leave. A grim smile worked his face as he sighted Justin Wardlaw seated in a green rocker on the hotel gallery, big hands resting upon his silver-topped cane. The man who believed money could buy him anything was sitting there secure in the belief that once again money had prevailed. He would never know how lucky he was that Ryan Coder had nursed a soft spot for victims of family breakdowns ever since his father had deserted him long ago.

He heeled the horse into a trot and slowly disappeared into the heat and haze of the West Texas Plains.

They pushed south at a steady pace, the heavy-shouldered manhunter in dusty brown and the ugly paint stallion that had carried him fifty miles in two days.

Jubal Creek lay behind them and the next stopover was Dunstan. Low, scrub-covered hills drifted by. It was hot and dusty with no living thing to be seen other than a solitary buzzard perched high on the dead limb of a cottonwood tree. This was badlands, the kind of country most men avoided but which was familiar territory to Ryan Coder.

The small daguerrotype of his quarry he carried had drawn no reaction in Jubal Creek. It was the same in Wilton, Millersville and Spanish River. And

Coder knew those questioned were telling the truth; he could always tell.

He stepped down in the shade of a rocky overhang. After seeing to the horse he hunkered down and drew the picture from his shirt pocket again. The three-year-old photo showed a handsome, smiling kid with a banner of light-coloured hair and a wild glint in the eye.

He reviewed what he knew of Danny Wardlaw; twenty-two years old, fair, blue-eyed, slim build, star-shaped birthmark on the right shoulder. Expert horseman, gunhand, brawler, drinker and maybe even outlaw with a preference for silk shirts and blonde women. Hot-tempered and almost certainly using another name – if still alive.

And missing three years.

It was an hour later when Coder buckled on the paint's saddle again then stood alone in the singing heat to stare southwards in the direction of the badlands. Down there lay Dunstan, Dime Box and Cheever County, leading eventually to the massive sweep of the Big Bend country and the Rio Grande.

With instinct to guide him he was heading steadily south. It was lawless country down there, a landscape of raw townships and mysterious trails with a thousand places a man could hide and stay hidden. Many of the killers and fugitives he hunted for a living eventually made for this rawhide south-western corner of Texas and Mexico sooner or later, and intuition told him his search for Wardlaw should begin there.

Absorbed in his thoughts he was less than fully alert as he walked back to untie his mount. The stallion butted his shoulder, almost knocking him off his feet. Coder cocked a big fist, but then grinned as he adjusted his hat and reached for the bridle. 'You'll keep, ugly,' was his mild reproof as he swung up and filled leather.

The horse kept darting wary glances back as they started off yet drew no response, for Coder was now lost in thought.

He was hunting a man whose only known offence was running away from home. He was not pursuing an infamous woman-killer like Ned Constantine, nor hunting some murderous bunch of desperadoes who'd proven too much even for the forces of law and order to deal with.

Just one young man who'd bolted and never returned.

Ryan Coder was searching for a lost son and brother and hoped this might prove to be the first of a whole series of jobs that didn't end with the stench of gunsmoke. He was looking forward to locating his man, returning him home then having the pleasure of forcing that good-looking sister to change her opinion of Ryan Coder. It was only when he realized how eagerly he was looking forward to seeing her again that he scowled and wondered what the hell that could mean.

From the back room of the Canasta Saloon Coder listened absently to the ceaseless murmur of voices and soft chink of glassware coming from the bar room. He reached out lazily to pick up his glass. Before him lay the remains of a hearty meal. A candle in a red glass globe filled the small room with a pleasant crimson glow. This was a place frequented mainly by lovers seeking privacy but was also an excellent spot for a trail-weary manhunter who simply needed to kick back and relax.

A soft knock sounded on the door. He transferred his glass to his left hand and rested the right on gunbutt below the level of the table.

'Come!'

It was the girl who'd brought him his meal of steak, tortillas, chili sauce and French fries. She was young and pretty but already showing signs of the buxom plumpness that so often came early to women of Spanish blood.

She enquired if he'd enjoyed the meal, and he nodded. She took her time clearing away the things, bending low over the table to offer Coder a generous glimpse of deep, creamy breasts. Then she stood with the tray resting upon a flaring hip, attempting to engage him in conversation. But his granite-faced silence soon discouraged her and she left, closing the door behind her.

Coder raised his glass to his lips. He'd bathed, shaved and changed into fresh rig before coming down to the saloon to ask questions and to eat. His black hair was brushed back from his forehead and his brown shirt emphasized the deep tan of face and hands. He felt rested following the meal, but not relaxed. His breed rarely relaxed in towns like Dime Box.

It was his first visit to the gloomy little Spanish-American outpost just north of the Rio Grande, and yet he was known there. He was known in most places where men who rode on the shady side of the law tended to gather.

On the street he'd sighted a man whose brother he had taken in once, and the fellow had recognized him. There was a saloon girl here who'd been in Hartley Gulch when he'd fought a deadly gun duel against outlaw Conway Dukes. By this, everyone would know who and what he was – Ryan Coder, manhunter. So . . . better beware!

Finishing his shot he rose and reached for his hat. He made his way along the narrow corridor that passed the galley where he glimpsed a wild-eyed Mexican cook wrestling with a growling black monster of a stove and cursing blasphemously as he opened the bar room door and stepped through.

He paused to take in the room. It was well-filled with the gambling tables doing good business and thirsty-looking *vaqueros* lining the main bar. A pair of drunks strummed guitars in a corner, their surprisingly fine playing conjuring up images of starry Mexican nights, sloe-eyed senoritas waiting for nights and lovers, ease, indolence and, of course, those sudden explosive outbursts of violence that were characteristic of Mexico. . . .

As he passed through he was aware of the reaction to a big gringo stranger with a tied-down pistol.

Suspicion, hatred and fear hung in the smoky air but affected him not at all. As he saw it, there were many worse things than being a manhunter. For instance, you could be a drink-raddled loser who quailed just because a big man with a tied-down gun riding his hip walked by. . . .

He reached the batwings as somebody called his name. He turned to play his gaze over the figures lining the bar until his gaze came to rest on the man in the yellow shirt.

His fingertips brushed the butt of his Peacemaker as he walked slowly back to the bar. The man named Dave Slater was young with a narrow pinched face dominated by bitter green eyes that had something loco lurking in their depths.

Outlaw.

Coder had struck Slater briefly in Skull Valley late last year while hunting rustler Tyrone Keep. The man was small-time yet dangerous. Back-shooting was his main talent.

'Slater,' he frowned. 'What brings you here?'

'Is that any way to greet an old friend?' Slater grinned, moving away from the bar with his right hand outstretched.

Coder ignored the hand. 'What do you want?'

Slater quit smiling. 'Still the same old Coder, eh? Still steppin' taller than any man's got the right.'

'Taller than you at least, Slater. OK, what is it?'

The youthful badman dragged the back of his hand over his mouth. 'Hear tell you're lookin' for somebody?'

'Correct. Feller by the name of Wardlaw. You ever strike him?'

Slater frowned thoughtfully. 'Name don't ring a bell. But they tell me you got a picture. He sounds kind of familiar, so mind if I take a look?'

Coder produced the daguerrotype. Slater studied the picture and glanced up sharply.

'This is Wardlaw?'

'Yeah. Know him?'

'Sorry . . . never saw him before in my life.'

Coder scowled as he slipped the photo away. 'You sure about that, Slater? I could have sworn you reacted when you saw the picture.'

'Never seen him in me life.'

Coder still wasn't convinced. 'I wouldn't take it kindly if I found out you knew something and didn't tell me, mister.'

The hardcase bristled. 'That a threat, Coder?'

'Yeah.'

They traded stares. Slater's bitter green eyes fell first. He turned sulkily back to the bar. 'I said I don't know nothin', Coder.'

Coder's big hand wrapped around the man's lean arm and Slater winced as he applied pressure.

'I'll find him if it takes a year, Slater. I'll find him, question him, and if I learn you do know him then I will come looking for you.'

'You don't scare me, big man!'

'If I don't then it just proves you're stupid.' Coder's fingers dug deeper into flesh until Slater cried out, and only then did he release his grip.

'Think on it, small-time. I'll be here until morning. If you recall anything come see me at the hotel. That could save you grief in the long run.'

Slater didn't respond. He stood massaging his arm with beads of sweat standing out on his narrow wedge of a white face. Coder cut a parting stare around the room then again made for the doors.

Only to find the girl who'd served his meal blocking his way.

'Señor Coder,' she smiled. 'Will you not stay and buy Rosa a drink?' Suddenly she leaned closer with her hands on his shoulders. 'Please, *señor*, Lily wishes to see you upstairs – something important.' She forced a brittle laugh and flipped his bandanna. '*Por favor*, handsome gringo? Just one little drink with Rosa . . . *por favor?*'

Coder surveyed the room. The drinkers were losing interest in them and returning to their tequilas. He looked at the girl and murmured, 'What does she want?'

'The picture. She knows something of it and says you are in danger.' Then she stepped back and said loudly. 'Well, if you will not buy me a drink then you are not the *hombre* I imagined you to be!'

'I'll buy you a shot anytime, Rosa,' an ugly drinker offered, and the girl crossed to him with a careless swing of the hips.

Coder stared after her expressionlessly before returning to the bar to buy a double shot. He drank and glanced up at the stairs. Lily Blaine was the only saloon girl he had known in Hartley Gulch. He liked her, would maybe even go so far as to say he trusted her.

He threw his shot down his throat and headed for the stairs.

CHAPTER 3

BLOOD JUSTICE

She wasn't pretty in a conventional sense, yet her figure was truly superb; long legs, full breasts, slender waist. Lily, obviously proud of her assets, sported an ankle-length gown of some filmy material which became transparent when she passed before the lamp.

The gunfighter was aware of those legs and the deep shadows and curves. Coder took his pleasures straight, yet whenever it came to a toss-up between business and pleasure, business won out.

After giving the girl his silent appraisal the manhunter moved off to a curtained alcove and flipped the drapes aside. It stood empty. He moved across to the windows and parted heavy curtains to gaze out. There was no balcony and the nearest door was a good hundred feet distant.

Satisfied, he returned to Lily who was studying him

curiously. 'You are a cautious man, Ryan.'

'Have to be.'

He appraised her again. She seemed determined to stand between himself and that ornate table lamp with the revealing blue globe which outlined her figure through her flimsy gown.

His eyes returned to her face. 'You on the level with me, Lily?'

Her eyes crinkled at the corners when she smiled. 'Don't you trust me?'

'I'm not sure. I get an urgent message to come up and see you, yet I find you wearing that dress and the look of somebody who isn't in an especially serious frame of mind.'

'Of course I'm serious. I simply wanted to look nice when you arrived, that's all.' A pause. 'Do you think I look nice?'

'Yeah . . . that's what you look . . . nice. So, let's get down to cases. What do you have to tell me about Wardlaw?'

She drew nearer, her expression serious now. 'Is finding him so very important to you?'

'Yeah.'

'How important?'

'Look, Lily, don't badger me about. I'm looking for Wardlaw and I mean to find him. That's plain enough, ain't it?'

'You're hunting him for bounty?'

'He's not wanted. I told you that downstairs when I showed you his picture. His old man is dying and wants to see him before he croaks. So now that we've got that straight, do you know him or not?'

She touched his arm and sighed.

'I was hoping I might persuade you to quit your search, Ryan, but I should have known better.' She took a deep breath. 'Well, perhaps when I have told you who it is you're after, you still might quit. I hope you do, for your own sake. I like you, Ryan. I've liked you ever since Hartley Gulch, and I would not want to see you—'

'Quit blowing on the fur and get to the hide, lady,' he broke in almost roughly. He was a man on the hunt, growing testy and impatient.

'Very well, Ryan.' She took a deep breath. 'The man in that photograph is Kid Silk.'

Coder stood motionless, black eyes fixed upon her face. Then he breathed, 'You've got to be mistaken about that.'

'I wish that were so. But I saw the Kid up close some six months ago when I was working in a saloon in Prieta. He came in with a gang looking for a man who'd informed on him to the Rangers.' She shuddered at the recollection. 'He was that man in the photograph, I swear it. Now perhaps you will understand why I am concerned for you and why I told Rosa to warn you of the danger you could be facing.'

Coder was puzzled. For amongst the many names to achieve colourful notoriety along the Rio Grande since the Civil War, that of Kid Silk held some prominence. He was also an enigma, and even Coder didn't know for sure if the man was a gunslinger, a cold-blooded killer or the most misunderstood young heller in the entire Big Bend country. The Kid allegedly carried a bounty of $5,000 upon his head but that, too, might have been just part of the myth.

This was his first hint Kid Silk and Wardlaw could be one and the same man.

He flicked the picture from his pocket and held it up before Lily's eyes. 'Take another look. A good look.'

'It's him,' she said without hesitation. 'He has barely changed since that picture was taken. You say he's twenty-two, yet he looks no more than eighteen. Fair hair, blue eyes, a big smile. That is him, Ryan. Kid Silk.'

Coder's memory kicked in at that moment. He recalled Libby telling him her brother had worn nothing but silk shirts from around the age of ten years. He knew nicknames often sprang from personal peculiarities or preferences. He himself was known as Brown Man Coder in some places due to the fact he always dressed in sober brown. . . .

He turned slowly away from the girl, his thoughts back at the ranchhouse at Mission where a dying man was awaiting the return of his son to brighten his last days – a son who just might prove to be a murdering outlaw!

He shook his head at this turn of the cards, and for a long moment was undecided whether to carry on with his search or return north and simply tell Wardlaw he'd failed.

He shook his head. He couldn't do that. He'd been hired to do a job and would see it through, like always. Wardlaw had contracted him to return his son to him, so he would do so.

'Ryan?'

He nodded and Lily went on. 'You'll still go on with it, I can tell by your manner.'

'Yeah . . . I'll go on with it.'

'I think you should consider more carefully. You see, I already know the Kid and his ways far better than you. You should know Kid Silk boasts friends, spies and contacts all over and if he knew you were hunting him your life could well be in danger. Why, he could be hunting you this very moment!'

He shook his head. Gossip, rumour and buffalo dust prevailed down here. He was prepared to see the Kid as a colourful character but the rest could be pure hogswill generated by the newspapers and saloon bar gossips . . . as most 'legends' proved to be, in his experience.

'Thanks, Lily,' he grunted. And reached into his pants pocket.

'I don't want that sort of gratitude,' she said when she saw the money in his hand.

Their eyes met and in hers he saw the invitation. She wanted more than money. Maybe she simply yearned for a little warmth and respect in her lonesome life, or then again she might simply be curious to find out if he really was the man of stone many claimed him to be.

But what was it Ryan Coder wanted and needed right now?

She read the answer in his eyes.

She reached out, his hand still in hers, and drew him down to the bed. Her free hand tugged at the tie cord of her gown and it fell open. Gently then she drew his dark head down. He felt the heavy swell of her breast against his face and his hands moved over her body inside the robe. Her fingers caressed over his muscular back, gently at first but then demandingly, nails biting into his flesh. Her body arched against him and she cried his name as she drew him to her.

The Canasta Saloon lay quiet and drowsing below him as Coder made his way along the upstairs hallway for the rear balcony.

He stepped out, fitted his hat to his head and glanced up at the sky. The night was clear with a lopsided moon sailing the high sky to the south above the Rio Grande. Ugly Dime Box looked almost pretty by moonlight and the sweet night smells of roses and grasses rose to him as he made his way down into the yard.

A fine night for riding.

He figured to make Cheever some twenty miles to the south-west by daybreak.

Cheever stood on the north-eastern tip of the Big Bend country upon a deep hook in the Rio Grande. The last information he'd had on Kid Silk placed him in the Cheever region someplace. He didn't expect to find him still there but it sounded like the place to start asking questions before heading deeper into the Big Bend.

The Big Bend was reputed to be a favourite stamping ground of the Kid's, which he was rumoured to share with innumerable other outlaws, drifters and border-sweepings who also found its wide-open spaces and almost total absence of law and order mighty attractive. 'The Cesspool of Texas!' a congressman had labelled the entire Big Bend recently, and that just about summed it up.

The rickety gate creaked as the solitary figure stepped into the alley flanking the saloon. Coder halted a moment to check out his gloomy surrounds before moving on, making for the main stem. Glancing upwards to where a faint blue window light showed, he blew a kiss and murmured, 'Thanks, Lily . . . for everything. . . .'

With the main street stretching away both left and right, he halted at the intersection to survey the nightscape before moving on. Men like himself attracted trouble like moths to the flame. As a consequence he was double-careful in dumps like this and was not for a moment forgetting what Lily had said about the Kid and his friends and spies. Funny, but he was now thinking of his quarry as Kid Silk, no longer as simply Danny Wardlaw.

The streets were deserted, with falsefronts and walks tinged with misty moon-silver. Coder hitched up his gunrig then moved out into the light and set off west in the direction of the hotel. It might be an idea to enter the stables and give the stallion a good slap across the snout before it could start acting up, he mused. For the one sure thing was that that paint horse was going to be sore about being saddled up at this godforsaken hour.

Then he heard it. The faintest rustle . . . one small sound which nonetheless seemed not quite right in this hushed night.

He threw his whole body fowards headlong with his right hand filling with Colt as fierce orange gunflame blossomed in the alley and a slug whistled overhead.

The detonation of the ambush gun merged with the thundering roar of his Peacemaker as the weapon loosed its own venomous blossoms of gunflame to pump lead into the phantom shape over against the wall. A man coughed and cried out and Coder triggered twice more, his firing trajectory dropping each time as he followed the falling shape to the ground.

Still locked in his crouch, Coder waited with a hunter's eyes scanning for other dangers in the darkness.

Then – 'Judas God. . . !' The agonized groan came from the man in the alley. He coughed once and was silent again.

Expelling breath, Coder went swiftly to the figure, his big body moving fast and quiet. He knelt by the sprawled figure and methodically replaced the spent shells in his Colt before reaching out to turn the man over.

'You bastard, Coder . . . I hope you burn forever in Hell. . . .'

'You small-timers never will never believe you're just born slow, will you, Slater?' he hissed. 'You've always got to find out the hard way.' Coder's tone was harsh and cold.

Dave Slater coughed red and a terrible spasm shook him. 'Gimme water, Coder.

'The hell with that. Why did you try to kill me?'

Slater's gaze managed to focus upon him, eyes bulging with pain and hatred. 'You'll never get him, Coder. He will dice your dirty liver for you. . . .'

'The Kid, you mean?' Coder guessed.

'He'll bury you . . . ohh, for God's sake gimme some water, Coder!'

'So, why'd you try and kill me, small-time? To make yourself a big man with Kid Silk mebbe? Tell me and you'll have all the water you want.'

'You dirty bastard. . . . Ahhh! All right . . . yeah! I fell out with the Kid and I figured if I got you he'd gimme another chance—' Slater doubled over as a fresh wave of agony gripped him.

Coder rose to loom over him, staring down without a glimmer of remorse or compassion. Slater would soon be dead with all that lead in him. . . .

Six-gun at the ready he turned away and headed for the street. He found it still empty. Nobody had been drawn out by the storm of shooting, not one curious face gazed from a window. Likely the citizens of Dime Box had heard guns at night often enough in the past to know the high danger of curiosity, and yet he could sense them watching him now from behind drapes and chinks in the walls.

44

He filled the crown of his hat with water at the nearby trough and returned to the gallery.

'Here,' he growled, kneeling at Slater's side. 'Here's your lousy water.'

He looked closer. Slater's eyes stared at the sky and he wasn't coughing any longer. Coder tipped the water from his hat and came erect.

'Small-timer!' he muttered, and turned away.

The night had begun well for Ellis Ramble.

'Come home drunk again tonight, you drunken, shiftless bum,' his fat wife had warned following supper, 'and you'll find yourself locked out with the dog.'

Only Ellis knew that such a threat simply indicated that Muriel was burning with lust and desire. So he'd quit their little love nest on the banks of the mighty Rio Grande secure in the certainty that no matter what time he returned the doors would not be locked and Muriel would not be asleep.

This had seemed a good omen for the night ahead and, sure enough, when the weedy little hardcase settled down at his customary table at the Little Dog Saloon the cards immediately began to run his way and he won forty-five dollars along with the mercenary heart of Juanita O'Brien – plus a lengthy political debate with Monroe Tolliver – all before midnight.

Then came the moment of decision. Should he push his luck with Juanita and the pasteboards – or make his way home to a waiting Muriel?

Home and hearth finally won out, for despite his triumphs at the tables he remained a weary man that night. Rustling stock could prove even tougher work than honest cowpunching and Ellis had just returned to home base from a profitable but exhausting cow-thieving job that had occupied three full days and nights.

So it had to be merely a tender goodnight to honey-lipped Juanita then the familiar track home-wards through the night streets of Cheever to his true love.

A cool breeze blew in from the river and the husky thief found it invigorating. He glanced at the moon and was smiling happily as he swung into the street leading to the river. Some days were diamonds – and this surely was one.

Ellis Ramble had no way of knowing he'd already squeezed every last ounce of goodness there was to be had from this over-long day.

Unblinking eyes followed his unsteady progress through the inky gloom of the old long-abandoned store shed. Coder had been hidden there, chain-smoking and pacing, ever since he spotted Ramble making for the saloon and arousing his interest.

He'd not seen the man before but his face was in the mental file of wanted dodgers he carried in his head; Ellis Ramble, rustler and horse thief, known associate of outlaws and fugitives.

Ramble, he had decided in a moment, would do just fine.

Coder had reached the outskirts just on dusk after

waiting the day out in the hills. He had his horse cached in a box canyon nearby now and was reassuring himself he simply wanted a lead or two from Ramble and hoped to get what he wanted the quiet way.

Ramble was moved to break into song as he approached the huge old shed with its rusted iron roof. His voice lacked quality and there was nothing really memorable about his lyrics as he sang:

The son of a bitch jumped over the fence,
Goodbye my lover, goodbye.
Slipped off a rock and swam for a week.
Goodbye, my lover, good—

The song broke off as the shadowy shape suddenly emerged from the black bowels of the old shed. Ramble blinked, strained his eyes to identify the hulking figure before him, slashed for the gun at his hip.

Coder lunged from the hips and his fist exploded against the hardcase's jaw. Ramble's legs buckled as fingers plucked the half-drawn Colt from his grasp. Though dazed, Ramble swung a whistling right at the head. Parrying the blow expertly Coder backhanded across the face, seized a handful of shirtfront then rammed the muzzle of his Colt up under a trembling chin.

'Relax and you might live until daybreak, Ramble!' he hissed.

Ellis Ramble drove his knee into Coder's groin

and filled his lungs to yell.

The shout was stillborn.

The edge of Coder's hand chopped across his windpipe and Ramble gurgled and half-choked. A fist ripped into his mid-section. As he staggered an upswinging elbow caught him a brutal blow to the side of the head followed up instantly by a left hook to the point.

His man wanted to fall but Coder wouldn't let him as he held him upright with one hand while pounding him with the other until he blacked out.

When he finally became conscious Ramble was sprawled on his back in the shed with a big boot at his throat. He made to struggle but quit the moment Coder threw chocking pressure upon his neck.

'Shut up, lie still and listen!' he ordered.

'For God's sake!' he gasped, suddenly scared for his life, 'what do you want, mister? If it's money, then I—'

Coder cut him off. 'I'm looking for Kid Silk and I figure a low-life like you would have to know where I could find him.'

'The Kid? Who knows anything about that cocky bastard? I—'

Coder's weight came down again and the helpless hardcase bucked like a sinner in torment.

'Do better, Ramble,' he snarled.

He thought his man was choking until he realized he was merely trying to get a name out before he strangled. Grudgingly, he eased the pressure on his neck and said, 'What? Speak up.'

'Cochilla!' Ramble got out, then coughed and cleared his throat. 'You . . . you know where that is?'

'Big Bend Basin, ain't it?'

Ramble's bullet head nodded. 'I never rode with Silk – and that's the mortal truth. But I have heard that's his hide-out town. . . .'

Coder squatted on his haunches considering the other's words. He sensed that Cochilla might have the right ring to it. Big Ben Basin lay some forty miles west of Cheever along the Rio, one of the great river's wildest sectors and so likely a logical place for somebody like the Kid to hang his hat.

After a time Ramble glanced up at him. The man's breathing had almost stabilized and he was no longer as scared as he'd been.

'Who are you anyway, joker?' he wanted to know. 'Are you John Law?'

Coder didn't respond; he was figuring how long it would take to reach Big Bend Basin. Ramble warily got to his knees, and when this brought no reaction, came fully erect. He looked like something a relay of hounds had dragged under the house.

'You through with me now, Coder? Er, can I go?'

Coder put a hard eye on the man as he straightened to full height. 'You'd never start hollering if I was to let you go, would you?' His face was epressionless.

'No, by God! I'd just figure myself lucky to be still alive, considering.'

'And you wouldn't think of mustering your pards and coming after me if I rode out – right?'

'Never!'

'The hell you wouldn't!' Coder drawled, then knocked him cold with with a perfect right hook.

It was twenty minutes before Ellis Ramble regained full consciousness and a further quarter hour to make his tangle-footed way home.

Up to the moment of that mule-kick king-hit to the jaw from Coder the hardcase had been planning to cut Coder adrift then raise the alarm and muster his bunch together to take the big man down, and so level scores with interest. Now his ambitions had shrunk. All he wanted was to gain the sanctuary of his lair, surrender to Muriel's tender care, then maybe lay up for a week.

But it just wasn't his night.

Upon reaching home on the moonlit banks of the river of rivers he found the door firmly padlocked. Muriel had waited up for him until midnight by which time her amorous mood was just a memory and the locks were being clicked shut. She heard him pounding on the doors, scowled venomously while she listened to his feeble story about being worked over by some mythical guntipper, then jammed pillows over her head to blot out the voice and drifted off to sleep again.

Alone in the night Ellis slumped on the stoop and a cool Rio breeze flapped his tattered shirt. A tidal wave of self-sympathy gripped him on what he'd considered earlier to have been one of his most promising nights. How far wrong could a man get? This had to be the worst night of his life. He shivered as that accursed Rio wind pressed his shirt against his body. He tried to warm himself by envisioning himself triumphant in a bloody get-square with Coder but for some reason it only caused him to feel colder.

CHAPTER 4

WILD MEN OF COCHILLA

The line of horsemen wound its way through the canyon country as the sun climbed blood-red out of the West Texas badlands.

There were ten of them, lean, hardbitten riders astride stocky mustangs which all showed the signs of long travel.

The pack had been on the trail almost a week, ever since word had come through to the Ranger station at Cobb City that cattleman Bob Tingle had lost five hundred head of prime steers. Now, ten days after the massive rustling raid, the Rangers had all but given up hope of recovering the Tingle stock but were still intent on running down those responsible.

Dust climbed the sullen sky in the still morning as the horsemen emerged from the mouth of a broad red canyon and glimpsed the Rio in the distance.

The Rangers had been following the course of the great river eastward for two days out of Amity now and at Amity had had their first real stroke of luck. Sheriff Wilson, who hadn't yet learned of the big rustling raid farther north, had an old drunk in his cells. The boozer was raving about the 'vision' he'd experienced one night a week earlier at his hut downriver. In this vision the derelict had seen the Rio Grande turn into a living sea of cattle which was being herded across by ghost riders from the north.

Immediately sensing that the old boozehound's dream might have in truth been stark reality, Ranger Captain Middleton had set about questioning the drunk and was eventually rewarded when the man had come up with a recalled description of 'A young jasper who didn't look old enough to be away from his mammy' actually leading his pack of night riders.

Middleton quickly realized the description he was being given of the raiders' leader tallied perfectly with his long-time outlaw *bête noire* – Kid Silk!

This told him that the Kid must have returned to his old haunts – and that was about as chilling as news could get along that outlaw-haunted reach of the big river.

The alarm was raised and combing the river regions the following day the Rangers' luck held when they crossed trails with a cranky old prospector-hermit from Big Bend Basin who, after soliciting several sizeable bribes, revealed his sighting of a pack of youthful horsemen crossing the basin and heading off in the direction of Cochilla.

Unlike the old boozehound the prospector had not been close enough to be able to furnish a description of the riders. Yet the fact they had been seen making in the general direction of Cochilla had proven sufficient to trigger Middleton into action. Middleton knew little about the mercurial Kid Silk, but one solid fact he'd gleaned about the boy rustler and hell-raiser since his climb to eminence in West Texas was that Cochilla was said to be one of his regular hangouts.

So the posse pounded swiftly eastward as a blood-red sun swung high above the mighty Rio Grande. Middleton knew how exhausted his men were yet dare not run the risk of stopping to rest when his quarry was possibly the most elusive, colourful and perplexing young hellion in a hundred miles.

The captain calculated, as they drummed towards the high red bluffs of the Rio, that they should reach Cochilla around midnight.

The hot day was dying as Ryan Coder rode down the steeply sloping cliff trail into Big Bend Basin. A yellow sun still seared the rocky ramparts of the basin wall, but it was gloomy down below here where the river lay like a sullen glowing snake against the shadows of the basin floor.

The sun was gone by the time the lone horseman reached the bottom where the swift Texas darkness enveloped him.

He halted to fashion a cigarette, protecting the

tobacco from the breeze by turning his broad back. The spurt of match flame briefly reflected in his eyes, keen, intent and watchful. For he was in strange country now, enemy territory. He was also alone by choice. He pushed on slowly, listening to the clip-clop of the stallion's hooves, his face tinged with crimson when he drew on his cigarette, a lone rider with a single mission. The Kid.

He knew who he wanted but still was a long way from knowing exactly what Kid Silk might be. Depending on who you spoke to, Kid Silk, aka Danny Wardlaw, was an innocent drifter-hellraiser bent on squeezing twenty years of boisterous living into three short years – or a lousy, back-shooting little outlaw who should have been tapped on the head at birth – with a mallet.

Stars began to lighten the gloom and now there was a glow to the south heralding the arrival of the moon. He'd hoped for cloud tonight but the vast sweep of the sky remained clear.

The moon peeped shyly over the high rimrock as he caught the tiny glimmer of light far ahead. He rode on steadily towards the great rocky ramparts which framed the dotted lights in the distance, nodding to himself when he realized just how the tiny town was situated.

Cochilla was built in a gulch with towering and almost vertical walls on three sides and the swift river replacing the fourth side. There was a bridge across the Rio here and it was immediately apparent this was the only way in. He nodded. He should have figured Kid Silk would be the kind to select a hideout town that could be so readily defended. Silk might well be young but plainly was no man's fool.

He finally drew rein a half-mile from the bridge. The construction was ancient and shaky-looking with a scattering of heavy boulders appearing to anchor it on the far side. Beyond those rocks the trail curved up and over a hill slope some two hundred yards in length before finally dropping into the town itself. From here Coder could glimpse only a rooftop or two, no lights.

His attention centred on the boulders. If sentries were posted that would be their logical spot. The river that came down from the north before angling south in the direction of the Rio Grande appeared both deep and swift. So the only way in would have to be by the bridge. . . .

He tethered the stallion to a cactus then checked out his Colt. No point in delaying now. He could sit here until daybreak and it still wouldn't look any easier or safer.

Gravel crunched beneath big boots as he started forward. Maybe there weren't any sentries, he speculated. This was remote country and owlhoots would have little to fear out here. In addition, he sensed Kid Silk shaped up as the cocky breed of young hellion who mightn't believe anybody would have the nerve to try and brace him right out here in his own bailiwick.

He focused on what his plan of action would be should he make it safely across that bridge.

He wasn't interested in tangling with any bunch of desperadoes here at Cochilla; he merely wanted Kid Silk. If he could first infiltrate the town and then lie low a spell, he might just get a chance to grab the Kid then maybe use him as a hostage to enable himself to quit the town in one piece.

And who could tell how it might pan out after that?

It could well be that when Silk realized Coder had been hired to find him and return him back home to his rich old daddy for what might likely be a death-bed reunion – not a rendezvous with a Northern hangman – the desperado might elect to go along with him peaceably. He could reason that inheriting a prosperous cattle ranch might prove an easier and safer way of getting rich than stealing other men's cows.

But of course by then it wouldn't make any difference whether Silk wanted to go home to Mission or otherwise. He would find out quickly that when Ryan Coder set out to get any man he always brought him back – one way or the other – be he innocent, guilty or someplace in between.

His steps slowed as he approached the bridge now. The moon had cleared the rim and cast deep pools of shadow around the sentinel shapes of gaunt grey boulders. Nothing stirred. Faintly, from beyond the silver-grey slopes, came the tinny sound of a piano. Coder stood staring at the river suddenly conscious of his strange reluctance to cross.

He knew why.

He had a sudden image of being forced to shoot it out with the killer who bore no resemblance to the splendid young son and brother his family imagined Silk to be. He'd have no option but to gun the Kid down then tote the carcass back home – thereby earning the everlasting hatred of both father and daughter.

'The hell!' he finally growled out loud, cocked the Peacemaker and started boldly across.

The shot crashed out the moment his boots hit the planking.

Coder hurled his big body violently to one side and punched a snap shot at the yellow burst of gunflame erupting from deep down amongst the boulders. A second gun opened up immediately and lead chewed the railing inches from his left shoulder. Coder touched off two more shots then rolled violently downslope before kicking to his feet. With bullets whistling viciously overhead he dropped into a low crouch and raced back the way he'd come.

Something grazed the side of his head just as his momentum carried him off the planking on to solid ground. He tumbled end over end, hat spinning from his head. For a moment he lay dazed and cursing with the landscape pitching and blurring in his vision. Then, realizing he'd only been creased, he kicked his way vigorously off the crown of the road just as a triumphant shout punctuated the reckless blasting of the guns.

'I got the big bastard, Darnell!'

'Finish him off!' another voice chimed in excitedly, and immediately a lean figure sprang up reck-lessly into full view from the rocks.

But though wounded and outnumbered the manhunter was never more dangerous. Belly-flat in back of a sturdy piñon now, gun outstretched to arm's length, he aimed deliberately and fired. The distant figure buckled and Coder's cutter flared again to hammer another slug into the body as it crashed to ground, face-down.

'You murderin' mongrel, Coder!' howled the single survivor who triggered wildly until a whistling slug powdered the crown of the base post, spraying him with brick dust and fragments.

Coder emptied his Colt at the gunflashes then sprang to his feet to cover ground in reaching strides. He'd put good distance in back of him before the ambusher's cutter chimed in again. A slug whis-tled high overhead, another slashed earth a good twenty feet to his right. Either this drygulcher had also been hit or else was the worst shot in Texas!

When another two bullets had missed him by a wide margin the gunfighter straightened up and concentrated solely on speed – and to hell with safety now. For a big man, Coder was fast. As pumping legs ate up distance he heard another shot whistle over-head, then moments later was plunging down the slope of the draw to where the stallion stood waiting.

Snapping the lines free of the cactus he filled leather with one giant leap and heeled hard. Startled, the paint leapt high and hit the ground running. Darting one glance back over his shoulder,

Coder glimpsed the figure crouched amongst the boulders and beyond him several running and shouting figures streaming over the crown of the slope from the town.

He explored his temple with his fingertips. The slug had merely scored hair and skin and clipped the top of his ear. There was plenty blood but nothing serious. His head ached and he reckoned he might be in for the grandaddy of headaches, but still knew he was damned lucky.

And maybe a tad unlucky as well ... or so he reflected as the first racing mile blurred beneath the stallion's hoofs. Unlucky he'd been recognized and identified as the manhunter.

Darnell was the name of the drygulcher who'd shouted his name back there. Quint Darnell was a young gunshark Coder had once booted through a store window in Taos Pueblo. He figured Darnell had identified him in the moonlight and had decided that Ryan Coder, gunfighter and bounty hunter, was not a man to be welcomed with open arms any place in Cochilla.

He didn't begin to relax until he'd put several fast miles behind. He was then content merely to savour the sweet taste of life for the moment and let the horse eat up big chunks of vital distance before glancing back.

No sign of pursuit.

That suited him just fine, for he was beginning to feel a little dizzy with the miles. He realized he'd need to rest up soon to stop the blood flow before he grew too weak.

A low hill rose off to his right. He steered the stallion towards it and reined in upon reaching the crest to check his backtrail again. The moonlight was weak yet he could still only make out movement near the bridge, a virtual guarantee nobody was pursuing him now.

This puzzled him some. But he didn't have the time or energy to think about it. Hipping around in the saddle he scanned the battered face of the basin wall immediately behind. There were caverns up there and they appeared accessible. The wall lay in such deep shadow that it would have to be next to impossible for the hardcases to see him climbing up there from that distance.

It would have to do.

It took twenty minutes to locate a suitable cavern, by which time a pounding headache plus blood loss were taking their toll.

Coder led the paint into a sizeable cavern where he off-saddled with some difficulty, then took rifle, saddlebags and water canteen out to the mouth of the cave where he hunkered down. First cleansing the wound with water, he unscrewed his whiskey flask and applied the spirits liberally, grimacing from the sting.

Next he took a clean shirt from the bags, ripped it into strips and wrapped it around his head, turban style. That done, he sat down and took a powerful double slug of the spirits and believed he was beginning to feel better until his surroundings appeared to be dimming.

He clenched his eyes shut, passed his hand across his throbbing forehead and opened his eyes again. The world was still gloomy. He gazed at the sky and realized a thin film of cloud had drifted across the face of the moon, grinned in relief. He wasn't about to black out after all.

With the rifle angled across his knees, he moved to wedge his back against the stone wall, stared out over the darkening basin. He attempted to think and plan but his mental processes weren't up to it. Maybe if he stretched out a spell it might take the mean kick out of this headache. . . .

His eyes closed and he settled into a more comfortable position. Time passed and the rifle began to slide off his thighs. The butt struck stone with a small, sharp sound. His eyes didn't open.

'I still claim we shoulda gone after him,' growled Rory Flynn, splashing amber whiskey into his glass.

'Which just goes to show how much brain you've got,' retorted Billy Tonkin. 'Not even Coder would have guts enough to come in here after us on his lonesome. It's my bet he's got a dozen men skulking out there with him someplace, mebbe more. The whole damned thing back yonder was a trap – a goddamned ambush.'

'Well, I don't give a rat's arse who's out there now,' put in flashy Chip Diamond. 'I reckon the only smart thing left to do now is hightail.'

An hour had passed since the firefight out by the

bridge. There were five youthful outlaws now lining the long bar of Cochilla's Cantina Riata. All looked worn and edgy, but one. Leaning lazily against the bar rail by the batwings and chewing on a blade of bluestem grass, Kid Silk's youthful unlined features showed nothing but contempt.

Maybe the Kid would concede the incident at the bridge had been a tad dicey. But the way they were carrying on about Coder a man could be mistaken into thinking they were talking about Old Scratch from Hades himself come to tote them off to Hell!

There was more to come.

'Quint told me once about the time he tangled with Coder in Taos Pueblo,' supplied Matt Beeber, sprawled against a table nursing the arm wound he'd sustained in the gunfight at the bridge. 'He reckons Coder worked three of them over with his dukes and then kicked their sorry backsides clear out of town.'

Beeber paused, rogue eyes widening even farther. 'And just because they was funnin' it up with some sportin' gal Coder happened to have his eye on at the time.'

'Hell, that's nothin',' chimed in Billy Tonkin. 'What about that time when Coder gunned down Sam Holder and Lee Conroy Crane in El Paso? Holder had seven notches in his Colt handle by then, and Crane was one of the fastest new guns in the trade.' He snapped his fingers. 'Gunned 'em both down in the main stem, so he did, and neither of 'em got off a shot.'

The Kid had heard enough. Give them another

hour jawing like this and they would have Coder taking on the US Cavalry – and winning!

'Goin' for a little pony ride, boys,' he drawled, strolling for the doors. He paused to grin mockingly as they stared in astonishment. 'Best you lock up tight while I'm gone, and maybe you should take shelter in the cellar. Who knows? Mebbe Coder ain't even human. The way you talk, he sounds like he could walk through walls.'

All began protesting at once but Silk silenced them with a curt gesture.

'Jumped up Judas!' he said disgustedly. 'What a bunch of yellow belly heroes I got myself saddled with! You ain't going to die without me for a spell.'

'So, where are you goin', Kid?' Rory Flynn asked nervously.

'Could be I'm gonna see if I can't nail myself a bogeyman,' Kid Silk grinned, and strolled out.

A brief silence in the bar room. Then there was a sudden clatter of boots as they hurried out on to the porch in time to see their youthful leader throw a leg across his mustang at the hitchrail.

'You're fixin' to go after that Coder, Kid?' Chip Diamond sounded awed. 'On your lonesome?'

'I'd take some of you with me only I'd be afeared your knocking knees might be heard all the way clear to the Rio,' came the sarcastic response. 'Keep sharp while I'm gone . . . and make a try at gettin' a grip on your nerves,' he snapped, then spurred away.

Heading for the bridge, Kid Silk was fully aware that it was all the scared talk about the manhunter that was driving him. The way they were reacting to Coder's name was like a red rag to a bull. There was but one man who rated that sort of respect, and his name was Kid Silk.

And riding down the long slope for the bridge in the gloom the gunman reasoned that his men had to be wrong about a planned ambush. To begin with, Coder had the reputation of a loner. Silk's instincts told him the big man was alone now – and there never was a single man he was afraid of. Sure, there would be a degree of risk involved. Yet the risk would be worth it a hundred times over should he get to nail Coder's pelt to the barn wall. Kid Silk was already a big name along the Rio Grande. To swing Coder's scalp off his belt would turn him into a legend.

He spoke to Burns and Tolliver standing sentry by the bridge. They had seen or heard nothing over the past hour. Silk rode across at a walk then hauled his six-gun before heading off for the draw where Coder had cached his horse.

He hadn't realized it was quite so dark until now. It wouldn't be easy reading sign in the poor light. He dismounted to study the imprints of Coder's horse, then swung up again to follow the trail at a walk. He'd last sighted Coder heading towards the east wall of the basin. He wouldn't bother sign-reading until he'd covered a couple more miles.

Eventually he reached the base of the slopes reaching up to the wall. He swung down to study the trail for sign. Several minutes later saw him hunker down, swearing softly to himself. The light was all but gone now but he could still dimly make out several sets of prints, although none clear enough to be certain which were Coder's. He daren't take the risk of striking a match.

He rose and studied the cliff wall. Maybe it would be best to ride up there and take a look around. The problem was that it would be impossible to climb that shale-littered face without raising a racket – which could prove to be like to handing his head to Coder on a platter.

Maybe a wider scout around down here would be smarter, he finally decided. If Coder had quit the regular trail, it should be simple enough to pick up his prints, despite the poor light.

The wide smile of Kid Silk flashed in the gloom as he turned and strode eastward. He'd covered some distance when something in the grass caught his eye. He knelt, squinted at the spot of colour, then smiled.

Blood.

Quickly he trotted back to the mustang, returned to the bloodstain then rode on. It was slow going, halting every few yards to study the earth for sign. But eventually he discovered another splotch of crimson and, a hundred yards farther on, yet another.

Eventually the tracks led to softer earth where it was possible for him to figure the direction the rider had taken leading away to the right, away from the trail. He followed the sign for some hundred yards until losing it on a wide shelf of stone. He found another stain on the shelf. Now he was sure. Coder had headed for the caves.

With a spring in his step Kid Silk went back to tie his horse to a tree. Then he double-checked his six-shooter, grinned up at the brooding cliff, and began to climb.

CHAPTER 5

ANGRY GROW
THE GUNS

Coder muttered in his sleep and attempted to shift his back into a more comfortable position against unyielding rock. The rifle lay at his side, like always. Within the cavern the stallion was dozing and maybe even dreaming on its feet, head drooping, hipshot. A foraging rodent slunk by across the broad plateau fronting the cave. The critter cut a sharp eye at the bulky figure of the man, then hurried on, sniffing.

The stallion lifted its head and once again Coder stirred. He half-awoke, shifted his cramped arm, and was drifting off again when he remembered. . . .

He jerked fully awake scrabbling for his rifle. Then the ache hit his temples and he clenched his eyes tight against it. The pain receded gradually. He hefted the rifle and the steel was very cold. How long had he been asleep? There was no telling.

On his knees he glanced at last at the silent cliffs, the long-shadowed sweep of the plateau, the bulk of a single pine that loomed darkly against a slowly lightening sky.

With a grunt he rose and stretched his heavily muscled body. He was cramped and sore yet realized immediately his head was much improved. Fingering the improvised strapping, he felt the dried blood. That was a good sign. If the bleeding didn't start up again he would mend fast.

He moved back into the cave to retrieve the whiskey. Suddenly he propped and turned, feeling his neck hair lift. There had been a sound. He waited, unmoving, but the sound was not repeated. But when he emerged again he caught a glimpse of a man's head and shoulders outlined above the curve of the plateau edge.

Coder dropped to one knee palming the Colt. Instantly, the distant figure ducked low and a burst of boreflame leapt out from his hunched bulk. The slug howled by Coder to ricochet off an unyielding granite wall.

The boom of his own six-gun almost deafened him as he fired back. He hurled himself to the ground headlong as his shadowy foe sent a shot back.

His trigger finger jerked twice and the billowing gunflashes poured through the gloom. He saw his lead strike sparks from stone and heard a wild yell. Deliberately, he pumped three rapid shots in the direction of the voice then dumped the Colt and dived forward scrabbling for the Winchester.

Lips skinned back from bared teeth now, the big gunfighter darted forward in a low crouch before propping to send a volley of shots across the open space, the tremendous volley of sound bouncing off the walls almost deafening.

The phantom gunman did not appear.

But Coder's blood was up by this and he flung himself forward across the plateau until a sudden clatter of stone from below the level of the rim halted him. A glance downwards sighted a slender figure leaping from boulder to boulder with the agility of a mountain goat. The Winchester butt slammed snugly into position against his right shoulder as the man glanced up. The light was poor yet he was still able to make out a youthful face framed by a shock of yellow hair tumbling like a banner across a high forehead.

'Wardlaw!' he bellowed. 'Hold!'

His answer was a bullet. Coder leapt backwards as the slug smacked hard off a rock then fluttered away harmlessly by him to fall spent in the grass.

He levered another bullet into the chamber and faster than the eye could follow whipped it up again to drive two whistling slugs between the fleeing gunman's boots.

Next instant Kid Silk launched himself into space and dropped from sight behind a gunmetal-grey outcropping.

Coder waited.

Eventually came the faint sound of receding steps and a split-second later he glimpsed the fast-moving figure vaulting a deadfall.

'Wardlaw!' he yelled again. 'I'm not out to take you in for bounty! Your father is dying. He sent me to find you!'

The answer was a gunshot even though there was no chance of a .45 reaching him at that range. This was plainly a defiant gesture to show what Kid Silk thought of his 'lies'.

Coder wheeled about and raced for the cave. He was flinging the saddle on to the stallion in preparation for the chase when he heard a volley of gunfire from far out across the basin.

'Busy night all round by the sound of it,' he muttered. Then, sweeping up his bedroll he quit the cave at the run.

Kid Silk was humming a tune and absently fingering the bullet crease in his shoulder when he heard gunfire from the direction of Cochilla.

He quit humming as he hipped around in the saddle.

What the hell was going on over there?

Yet immediately he began to relax again, his frown vanishing. Jittery idiots shooting at shadows, was his guess. Whoever it was would have heard the gunplay from here and it had made them jumpy and jittery. Some bunch of hardcases! He'd have plenty to say when he rejoined them.

The Kid was solid ready to give somebody a mouthful as he kicked the mustang into a lope. Anybody would do. The light flesh wound was nothing yet the damage to his vanity was of far more concern.

For tonight Coder had driven it home that Kid Silk might just not be quite the king of the Colt 45s he'd reckoned himself to be.

Coder just might be better!

That was one hell of a thing to have to admit and a chill ran through him as he fully realized how close he'd just come to getting killed before he'd had the sense to hightail.

The boys were right when they claimed Coder was unbeatable. Yet he believed himself still to be craftier, meaner and smarter than any manhunter hick could ever be. He was so crafty in truth that the majority down here still looked upon him as a handsome, personable boy all the girls were crazy about. His personality was that persuasive. He might have simply vanished with Coder's appearance to surface later after he'd gone and resume his double life as dashing Kid Silk and the hellraiser with the gun.

But Coder had shaken him and he was committed to take him down.

His surge of confidence was quickly replaced by harsh reality, however, as the mustang carried over a rise in the trail to bring the town abruptly into view. The heavy cloud cover had blown away in the past few minutes and he could clearly make out the distant shapes of horsemen upon the bluegrass slopes beyond the bridge.

His eyes narrowed as he reined the mustang back to a slow lope. Were those his own men mounted up over there? And, if so, why?

Something cold touched the Kid's heart as he drew closer. He could still hear the distant snarl of guns from the town and realized his guess about the men shooting at phantoms had to be off-target. There was something plainly very wrong over there.

Another quarter mile and he dragged his mount to a stop. A horseman had appeared over the lip of the town slope, followed closely by a pursuer. He saw the gunflash before the crash of the shot reached him. The first rider pitched from his saddle and went rolling over and over towards the river. He realized the riderless horse that came clattering across the bridge was a palomino – Chip Diamond's horse!

There was a taste like dry dust in the Kid's throat as he watched the man who'd gunned Diamond down turn and go racing back towards the town. It was only too plain now that Cochilla was under full attack.

There was no sign of activity in the area surrounding the bridge now, only Diamond's still shape upon the bank and two further lifeless figures, one at either end of the bridge.

Edgy and ready to turn back at the first sign of danger, Kid Silk moved on slowly at first but soon impatiently kicked into a gallop. The sounds of shooting had largely died away by the time he had reached the bridge.

Gun in hand he approached the first body.

His eyes snapped wide when he saw the Ranger's badge pinned to the dead man's chest.

For a bad moment the Kid was too stunned to think straight. First Coder then the Rangers – both in one night! As his numbed brain was finally beginning to clear, he heard a distant shout from beyond the rise.

'Hold your fire, men! That's a white flag they're waving from the window!'

Kid Silk slowly turned his horse back the way he'd come. He could scarce believe what was happening. They'd defied the law here with ease for so long yet within the space of an hour it was all over.

And if he hadn't gone out there after Coder it would have been all over for himself as well. . . .

He kneed his mustang into a trot and headed south. He didn't look up for a time and when at last he did the first thing he sighted was the lone rider lifting a cloud of dust a half-mile distant.

Coder!

All too plainly the danger was far from over just yet.

A light pressure of the knees moved the mount into a gallop again and saw him go sweeping across the basin floor headed the west wall of the canyon. He had to get out of this stinking basin fast! With Coder almost within rifle range and a troop of Rangers back in Cochilla, this was no place for him to be right now.

But where to go?

He could make it across the Rio Grande yet knew the Mexican side was crawling with *Rurales* right now, most of the sons of bitches out hunting for him.

Black Butte was always a good hideout but was near fifty miles from here. Brushy Gulch? Thirty miles east along the Rio Grande and deep in the heart of the thorny brush country. It didn't appeal right off yet the further he rode, and the clearer he saw the danger he was in here, the more obvious the solution.

His head bobbed emphatically. Brushy Gulch it was!

In a half hour he'd regained the wide-open country where he veered east under a brilliant moon. He was long gone from sight by the time the big-shouldered man astride the paint stallion emerged from the pass . . . yet the tracks of his passing were vividly etched in the red dust.

Coder followed them around this unnamed bend in the Rio Grande.

Coder stood by his horse.

The morning sun struck the earth with a brassy glare and sent heat waves upwards against his face. There was no wind, the whole panorama seemingly frozen; brown grass, motionless brush thickets, the arching purple of this southern sky and shafting sunlight shimmering across the mighty valley of the Rio Grande.

Eventually he stirred.

He unbuckled his water canteen, soaked his kerchief in it, then held it to the stallion's mouth. The horse sucked on the cloth, watching Coder with an accusing eye. The animal knew the river was close by and could not understand why he wasn't being taken down there to drink his fill.

Replacing the canteen Coder adjusted his head strapping. He took another swig from his dwindling whiskey supply then sat up more erect to survey his surrounds again. Nature was strong on uniformity along this wide bend in the river. No matter where you looked it was brush – trackless, empty, lifeless brush.

He shook his head.

Might as well admit it, Coder.

Silk's given you the slip.

Were he familiar with this stretch of country he might have guessed at his quarry's destination during this long run from Big Bend Basin. Yet even had that been the case, he brooded, he still would be unable to take advantage of such knowledge. For he'd ridden the paint all out without making any impression on the Kid's runty mustang. Then the Kid had quit the basin with a long head start and had finally lost him here.

Coder squinted at a climbing sun and calculated he'd been standing here for an hour or more, too weary to keep hunting and too mule-stubborn to quit.

Common sense told him to turn and make for the closest town yet stubbornness proved stronger. He sensed there would be no quit for him until he'd combed this entire vast sweep of brushland end to end ... and momentarily pondered whether this indicated strength of will or sheer stubborn stupidity.

Whatever the answer he would stick to the trail – if

there was one. But plainly the first thing to do was to ride down to the river, water the stallion then cook up a decent breakfast chow.

Brushy thorns plucked at his chaps as he led the horse for the ridge which hid the Rio from sight. The dull ache in his head was less severe now and he knew this would improve after a plate of fried jerky and plenty hot coffee.

He climbed the ridge slowly, feeling the sun burning through his shirt. It was shaping up to be another hot one – although nothing the Texas sun cooked up could be half as hot as things had been back there at Big Bend Basin. He wondered what all that gunplay had been about in Cochilla. He'd half expected to sight Silk's riders coming after him when he'd trailed the Kid from the basin, but maybe all that gunplay he'd heard likely suggested the outlaws had had troubles enough of their own in the town.

Suddenly he propped.

The clear sound of a gunshot had breached the morning hush. His eyes narrowed to a single steely gleam as he played his gaze east over a sea of brown brush. For a brief time all was still. Then two more shots sounded in rapid succession and moments later he saw kicked-up dust rising from a deep gulch less than half a mile south.

Slamming boot into stirrup, he swung up. The dust cloud was lifting high now and he caught a fleeting flash of movement deep within the thickets.

He waited.

The shooting had stopped to be replaced by

shouting distorted by heat and distance. He focused upon the base of a rising dust cloud. Somebody was storming through that section of brush on horseback at the gallop. He caught fleeting glimpses of horse and rider and after several moments the rider erupted into clear sight to go storming across an open patch of ground before the brush swallowed him again.

The horseman was Kid Silk and, judging by the larger dust cloud following him, he had company.

Coder continued to wait motionless, heels lifted from the stallion's flanks, ready to rowel him into a gallop. Kid Silk was still drumming westward on a line parrallel with the ridge that was bringing him closer to the watching gunfighter with every stride. Coder wanted to buy in, but first he needed to know just who or what the Kid had coming behind him.

He found out in a hurry when a pack of big-hatted riders came plunging across that open space brandishing rifles with bright sunlight striking points of fire from the crossed ammunition bandoliers slung across their chests.

He'd counted eight riders before the last man flashed from sight. He nodded soberly. Bandidos from across the Rio, if he was any judge.

Instantly Coder put the horse to the gallop and struck off at a tangent to the ridge which would eventually cut Kid Silk's line of headlong flight. He thought that maybe the running man deserved whatever it was those greasers seemed hell-bent on dishing out to him – but the Kid was his!

Intent on the trail he was following at breakneck speed the Kid failed to see the big horseman homing in on him from his left flank until Coder erupted from the brush cover, almost atop him. Silk's jaw sagged in shock as Coder came hammering up alongside him. The man's right hand flew downwards but Coder's Peacemaker swung up to fix squarely on his face.

'Don't try it, Kid!' Coder shouted as both ducked low beneath the branch of a tree.

'Fry, you bastard, Coder!' the outlaw snarled, yet with both hands working the reins again. 'Go ahead! Shoot and be damned! But you'll have to be quick if you don't want somebody else to beat you to it.'

The brush was beginning to thin now as Coder cut a swift glance back over his shoulder.

'Who are these Mexes, Silk?'

Kid Silk actually laughed. 'My old pard Benito. You've heard of him, no doubt?'

'Right . . . rustler scum from below the river. But what's the play?'

'What the hell does it matter?'

Side by side they went hammering across the final brushy level then the open country suddenly lay before them, the shimmering trace of the Rio Grande now a mile to their left.

'I want to know, Kid!' Coder bawled after they'd covered a hectic quarter-mile.

'So, I crossed the greasy bastard on a little deal,' came the panting reply. 'Must've figured I would show up around here sooner or later and they were

79

laying for me when I rode in. Only trouble for them, Benito had to make a big speech first before he rubbed me out.' That reckless smile flashed. 'I blasted two of the sons and got away without so much as a crease!'

Coder again glanced back trail. Although losing ground the Mexicans were in clear sight now, every swarthy face angry and intent as they used hands and heels searching for greater speed. He turned ahead, eyes sweeping over the river before finally playing north.

'I'll make you an offer!' he yelled at length. 'I'll help you shake the greasers if you agree to hand over your Colts when we're in the clear.'

The Kid shot a glance back to see nothing but angry men with guns.

'OK, a deal, big man. What have I got to lose?'

'Nothing but your life,' Coder muttered. Then he gestured ahead. 'What do you favour? Stick to the river or try to swim it back to Texas?'

'Can that fleabag of yours stay?'

'Good as any.'

'Then let's stick to the river and outrun the miserable sons of bitches!'

So they raced east and followed the bends and sweeps of the big river. They kept to a dead run as the miles flowed beneath flashing hoofs and a fierce sun climbed the sky. For an hour their pursuers hung on grimly but when the terrain roughened into a series swaybacked ridges and gully washes, the bandidos finally began to lose valuable ground.

'No bottom to them greaser cayuses!' Silk laughed as they plunged along a steep-walled draw then fought their way up the far bank. 'Always tried to warn Benito he should trade them pokes for a bunch of good old Texas cow ponies, but that pilgrim ain't smart enough to come in out of the rain!'

The whole business plainly seemed like one huge joke to Kid Silk but if there really was any humour in the situation it was lost upon Coder.

They were opening up a healthy lead by this, but were far from clear just yet.

The Mexicans were dogged hunters, and Coder had heard enough about Benito to know what they might expect if they failed to make good their escape.

It was hot by this and the horses began to labour. Their way led across a vast slope studded with mesquite, chapote, bluethorn and cactus. On topping out a crest they could look back to sight their pursuers a good mile or more behind now, strung out in a ragged line.

Turning ahead, Kid Silk shot a triumphant smirk at Coder, which faded next moment when he stood in his stirrups to stare at a billowing dust cloud rising some two miles dead ahead!

Coder sighted the dust in the same moment. The two exchanged a glance and reined their horses back to a lope. A short time later the squad of riders reappeared outlined against the clouds of their own hoof-raised dust, and Kid Silk jerked his mount to a dead stop.

'Rangers! I don't believe it!'

Coder's mount stopped on a dime and the rider shoved his hat back off his face. Now it was plain to see the sunlight glinting off the lawmen's breast badges. He was absorbed with what he was seeing before he twisted sharply at the sudden stutter of hoofbeats.

The Kid was driving his horse headlong for the river!

Instantly Coder gave chase, jaw muscles working under bronzed skin as he lifted the animal to a full gallop in the Kid's dust. There had been no intention of fording the Rio Grande and taking their chances with Mexican law up to this point, but sight of that menacing dust cloud yonder suddenly caused Old Mexico to sound like the ideal destination.

Coder rode hard but the outlaw's barrel-chested mount hit the water well ahead in a huge burst of spray, plunged deep momentarily then surfaced to start swimming strongly for the Mexican shore.

Silk raised his boots up on to the horse's neck and Coder heard his laughter above the deep roar of the river. He could tell simply by the way that animal handled the current that the critter had braved this river before as it plainly held no terrors.

The same didn't apply to his stallion. Coder's paint was a dry country animal and some of horse and rider's most memorable battles had been fought in the past when Coder wanted to swim a river which the stallion was scared of. But he wouldn't tolerate any temperament today, so as they approached the spot where Silk had gone in Coder raked with spur and virtually lifted the animal over the last low sandstone ledge and plunged headlong into the water.

They hit hard and water surged around Coder chest high with the horse totally submerged beneath him. But only briefly. The paint's head broke the surface and it began to swim erratically, the current bearing them downstream. The rider patted the animal's neck in an attempt to calm him, but though swimming more strongly now they were still being borne well below the line Silk was following.

By the time Coder had reached midstream Kid Silk's mount was searching for the bottom with pumping hoofs some seventy-odd yards upriver.

A quarter-mile to the west, the Ranger patrol had reined in upon a bluff. Coder caught the glint of sunlight on binocular glass as a rider put the instrument to his eyes.

Downriver on the Texas side Benito's wild bunch had also halted at the water's rushing edge. The *bandidos* were waving their rifles furiously in frustration but the rich Spanish invective they directed at their fleeting quarry was lost in the voice of the big river.

Coder blanked his mind to all else as the stallion swam strongly now although still buffeted by the sheer power of the current. Meantime Silk was making headway for where the bluffs were both low and long. Directly ahead of Coder, however, the bank still reared steeply. Nor was that the only challenge. Above the voice of the river could now be heard the muffled sound of a repeater rifle followed by something plopping into the rushing water close by.

He was drifting into range of the guns!

He hurled himself out of the saddle and seized hold of the stallion's tail. Free of the weight on its back the animal's stroking improved until shortly Coder felt them finally break loose of the main current. The banks loomed closer and he could no longer hear that ominous sound of bullets smacking water. Twisting his head, he saw that Kid Silk had kicked free of the river altogether to crest a high bank some two hundred yards upstream, his slender figure silhouetted against an innocent sky. The outlaw threw him a mocking salute, kicked the horse once and dropped from sight.

Coder cursed and water filled his mouth. But almost in the same moment he felt the horse's hoofs at last strike bottom, and suddenly they were surging up the sloping bank.

Once free of the water's grip Coder pulled back hard on the stallion's tail, then lunged forward to seize the trailing lines. In the saddle again, he set the horse to the bank. He felt its shoulders pumping as they laboured upwards and then surged over the lip to reach level footing.

Kid Silk by this was a fast-receding shape through a wind-blown cloud of dust well upstream.

'Yeeeahhhh!' Coder roared, and kicked the stallion into a gallop yet again.

His next glimpse of his quarry showed the Rangers also following the outlaw's progress as he closed in swiftly on a belt of timber. But by this Coder was charging after him and was plainly gaining ground despite the quality of his good horse. Yet hardly had this thought registered than the distant riders began shouting and gesticulating wildly towards the timber belt.

Coder's eyes narrowed as he tried to figure what was attracting their interest. His eyes cut to slits of concentration as he focused on the treeline to detect movement. But before this could be identified Silk's racing horse suddenly went down as if its legs had been slashed from beneath it.

One second later Coder heard the flat report of a rifle and jerked the stallion to a halt.

A phalanx of black-hatted horsemen had erupted from the woods and now were galloping furiously towards the downed outlaw.

Rurales!

Coder sat his saddle with hoof dust drifting away from him and sudden deep lines of both exhaustion and disappointment cutting his cheeks. To have gone through all he had done over the past twenty-four hours only to have it end this way seemed the final, brutal irony.

So he watched, numb with frustration and weariness as the Mexican police swarmed around the outlaw . . . before realizing two black-hatted riders were now staring and pointing his way.

He swung about and rode back the way he'd come. When a rifle crashed, he used his spurs. A *Rurale* trio broke away from the main bunch and started after him until a shout from their officer recalled them. The *Rurales* already had what they wanted; they had Kid Silk.

But what did Coder have? Nothing but the bitter taste of a failure which it would take a lot of tequila to wash away.

CHAPTER 6

RED RUNS THE RIO

The small dark-headed Mexican boy watched the old man bait his fishing line, then turned his eyes to the river. In morning sunlight, the Rio Grande to him was like a great ocean, curving away, broad and red and turbulent beyond the jetties of San Prieta.

'Old one?'

'*Sí*, little one?'

'Where does the river go?'

The old man smiled. He was brown and vastly wrinkled, yet still spry. For seventy, maybe eighty years, he'd nurtured the belief that the big river would protect him and keep him from the grave, providing he never left its side. He was in for a rude shock somewhere in the near future but today his faith was strong as ever.

'Where does it go, you say? Why, it goes forever, Pablo.'

'Is forever a place, Grandfather?'

'It has to be, for that is where the great river flows.'

The powerfully built American seated upon the pier in the shade nearby, nursing a hangover, shook his head and stared hard at the old man.

'That's no way to educate a kid,' he growled. 'Why don't you answer him honest?'

Emiliano looked at the American with mild eyes. 'It is the truth, *señor*.'

'Hogswill!'

The ancient one smiled indulgently. 'I say the river flows forever . . why? Well, it was here in my father's day, and his father before him. I read the great books of Mexico that say the river was here before light, before the sun itself . . . and I believe because I wish to and because it makes me happy. But you? You do not believe and you are unhappy.' He spread his gnarled hands. 'Which belief is stronger?'

Coder scowled. A man should know better than to try and talk sense to anybody this side of the border, he told himself sourly. Yet almost immediately, watching the old man and the child laughing together, he was realizing the old timer was likely right, after all. For surely he was happy while Ryan Coder was not.

But as he rose to stand and swing his arms for circulation he could at last feel the hangover beginning to ebb. Should be gone by noon, he predicted. Then by two o'clock he would likely feel healthy enough to buy himself a drink. One shot.

He'd been worn down and jaded by the time he'd stopped off at this nameless dot upon the great river. He'd needed a good blowout, had enjoyed it, now couldn't shake off the after effects quickly enough to suit.

He was pacing up and down by the riverside some time later when the old man approached again. Coder gave him the fish eye but it was ignored. Seemed this old geezer loved all mankind, even hungover manhunters who'd just managed to lose an outlaw worth genuinely big dollars to the American law – for anyone smart enough to bag him, that was.

Coder liked to regard himself as smart but right now the facts didn't support that notion. For overnight the *Rurales* had somehow snared the Kid and doubtless would very swiftly get to hang him high, wide and handsome. He was objective enough to concede he wasn't looking any too smart, all things considered.

'The young one says you told him you are a lawman, senor?'

'I didn't say that . . . exactly. I said I was hunting an outlaw and he got away. That doesn't make me law.'

'You hunt men for money?'

'What's wrong with that?' His hangover was stirring again.

'I know the one you hunt,' came the sober response. 'Very bad. *Mucho trabejo* – much trouble.'

'That sounds like the Kid all right.'

'Kid Silk?'

He glanced up sharply. 'You know him?'

'I know of him,' the old man conceded, measuring him with his gaze. 'He is bad for Mexico and for your country also.'

Coder shrugged, bored with the conversation already. 'Tell me something I don't know.'

'Do you know where this one is now . . . with the *Rurales?*'

'Look—'

'I know many things, *señor.*'

The hangover was almost gone he realized, and this old geezer suddenly appeared sharper than he'd had him figured.

'All right . . . he's being held in Pierro,' he growled.

'Ahh, Pierro. Then he would be in the hands of Captain Antonio Robles, would he not?'

'That's what I hear.'

Vallinova spread his hands. 'In that case things may not be as bad as you think, *señor.*'

Coder scowled. It could be the last of the hangover messing up his thinking, he supposed, yet the more this oldster said the more he seemed to shape up as something more than just an ancient river rat.

He said, 'Do you know anything or are you just pretending, Pops?'

A chuckle. 'Ahh, you suspect now that perhaps the old one has some wisdom, no? Well, as I hate all the evil ones who come to our sad land, and because I look into your face and see mostly good, I will maybe assist you. But first I must warn that in encouraging you to perhaps follow what I say and by so doing come to grief or even your death, I must be—'

'Don't bore me to death, old man,' Coder cut in. 'If you reckon you can help, and aren't just whistling Dixie, then let me hear it.'

'Very well. But first, do you have money?'

'Ahh, so you want *dinero*? I should have known—'

'Señor, it is common knowledge that Captain Robles of Pierro, although a man of much courage and achievement, would sell his own mother into bondage to the Indians if enough gold crossed his desk. Do you wish me to continue?'

Coder nodded. He wished, right enough.

'Very well. As I say, to Robles money is all. I do not know if he would hand over this gringo outlaw for gold, but I do know he has done such things in the past. But perhaps you do not have enough—'

'Let me worry about that, Gramps,' he cut in. He scented something in what the old man was hinting at, something that might prove valuable. Maybe he could help him bust a man out of a Mex jail? It would be anything but the first time such a thing had happened south of the border.

At moments like this the manhunter was quite capable of going overboard. He didn't see it that way. His trade was motivated partly by profit but largely by committment. He hated outlaw scum with a passion and Kid Silk, for all his boyish charm, possibly fitted that category; who could be sure? To leave him in a Mexican jail could see him either buy or bust his way out. But if he delivered him for the money on his head north of the Rio the law would at least be given its chance to try him and find him guilty or innocent.

'Just believe I've got enough *dinero*,' he said after a silence. 'Now, why don't you tell me everything you know about Pierro, Captain Robles and whatever else might be cooking in that old grey head, Grandpa.'

So they talked on and by the time the old man was through Coder's hangover was gone and he was fishing his billfold out of his hip pocket.

But the man thrust the proffered bills away. 'I have no use for money, *señor*. One of the great advantages of growing old is discovering there is so little one really desires. And who knows? Perhaps I have not done you any kindness today? Perhaps you will die in Pierro and they will steal your money and then dump you in a pauper's grave?'

Coder's rare smile showed. 'I'm hard to kill. Mebbe like you?'

'Life is but a short thing no matter how long you live. Good fortune, *señor*. Go with God.'

They talked quietly for ten minutes before Coder saluted and started up the slope in back of the jetty. He paused to look back down upon gaining the crest. The old man was seated at the child's side again, their figures silhouetted against the broad, sparkling sweep of the river some claimed had flowed forever.

He turned away and headed off for the livery stables on the river town's tiny central square.

The big leather chair creaked as Captain Antonio Robles sat down. That chair was the *Rurale* captain's most treasured possession. Elaborately carved and highly polished, it had come originally from far Mexico City where it had once occupied pride of place in the palace of the Emperor Maximilian. It was uncomfortable and to sit on it for any length of time was a penance, yet it had real authority.

A slender, dapper man with pencil-line moustache and sharp, shrewd eyes, Robles selected a golden cigar from a silver case. He clipped off the end and reached for his matches. He studied Coder over the tiny flame, sucked the stogie into full life then leaned back comfortably.

'Surely a single virtue I have always admired above all other has been courage,' he murmured. 'Yet courage so often goes hand in hand with foolhardiness, Señor Coder. Would you not agree?'

Coder just shrugged. He sat directly across from the Mexican in a more ordinary yet very comfortable chair. His holster was empty. In back of him, a swarthy *Rurale* stood on either side of the door to the captain's office. Each man toted a rifle in the crook of his arm.

Robles watched the thin column of smoke climb from the cigar. 'To be brave is honourable, to be fool-hardy, dangerous. Yet to lie could prove suicidal. Perhaps you would agree to that, *señor*?'

'I haven't lied to you.'

'But of course you have. All this business about the man Silk being the son of a rich gringo who contracted you to find his son and bring him home – lies!'

'I could prove you're wrong, given time.'

'Ahh, but time can be so short, gringo. Short for both Kid Silk and possibly you.' Robles leaned forward. 'Do you take me for a complete fool, gringo? You come here and offer a bribe for Silk's release, yet your offer is so laughable it can only mean you are attempting some kind of trickery or subterfuge. . . .'

'Two hundred dollars ain't any kind of pittance in my book.'

'Pittance!' the man behind the desk reiterated. 'You seek to buy Silk for $200, then return him to Texas law where there is a $1,000 reward on his head. You realize, of course, that we are well aware that you are a professional bounty hunter? Your record was known in this regard even before we captured Silk, who then merely confirmed it.'

'How much?'

'Pardon?'

'How much do you want for Silk if $200 isn't enough?'

Robles' eyes narrowed. 'There is more?'

'There could be. Look, Robles, just take it as truth for a minute that Silk's father paid me a retainer to hunt for and rescue his son – and that is what I'm now offering you. But seeing as you're kinda greedy maybe I could contact Wardlaw and see if I can't get him to up the ante. But I'd need a figure first. What's the lowest amount you'd take to turn him over to me?'

'By the Virgin, Coder, if you are a liar you're a

convincing one.'

Robles rose to pace the room, slapping his thigh with a leather quirt. He paused to scowl pensively at his blank-faced bodyguards, then came slowly back to his desk. 'All right. Nothing less than one thousand dollars would compensate me for what I would lose in respect and dignity should my prisoner "escape".'

'Hmm . . . still a lot. . . .'

Coder was still acting but Robles was not when, following an impatient wait for a response for just a few seconds, his restraint snapped.

'Your response, scum!' he shouted.

The Coder temper flared then. 'Takes one to know one!'

The quirt flashed and struck, leaving a weal across Coder's cheek. He saw red and lunged at the man behind the desk but froze when rifle hammers clicked in back of him.

'Pure gringo scum,' Robles reiterated softly, bending the quirt between his hands. 'Yet I do believe we understand one another now, Coder. Of course, I could have you dragged out and shot like the mangy scum you are, but profit is always more important to me than watching dead men being dragged from my courtyard. You are free to go. If you fail to return with my one thousand dollars in twenty-four hours, Silk will be executed. And should you fail to appear, you will eventually join him. Get out!'

Coder picked up the hat he'd bought in Pierro. His face stung but he did not finger the weal. He would not give Robles that satisfaction.

'I'll be back,' he stated flatly. 'But before I go, I want to inspect the merchandise.'

'I do not understand?'

'Silk. I need to know he's still alive.'

Robles shrugged and suddenly looked bored with it all. 'As you wish. Guards, take him to view the prisoner. Watch him closely.'

A guard opened the door. Robles slammed his desk top with the stick. 'Twenty-four hours, gringo vermin!'

Coder turned and walked out. The two *Rurales* fell in behind and conducted him down a long, gloomy corridor then out through a massive cedar door and into a courtyard.

The harsh smash of sunlight was an assault on the eyes after the cool gloom of Robles's office. A bunch of *Rurales* seated in the shade, smoking, watched them go past to reach the squat adobe building which was the prison for the headquarters. The far east end of the building was eroded and deeply pitted with bullet holes. Ugly brown stains spattered the wall. The citizens of Pierro had grown so accustomed to the sudden outbreak of gunfire from this place they no longer even paused to cross themselves at such times.

A gross jailer with an enormous black moustache admitted them to the stinking prison. The guards escorted Coder to a gloomy back cell. He looked in to see Kid Silk stretched out upon a narrow bunk puffing on a cornhusk cigarette.

'Well – shoot!' the Kid grinned, swinging his boots to the cell floor. 'If it ain't the big man and nonesuch wonder himself!' White teeth flashed as he came to the barred door. 'Hell, never thought they'd get to run you down, Coder.'

Coder was impressed. It seemed nothing could succeed in rubbing the flash shine from Kid Silk.

'You OK?' he grunted.

'Never better. Say, where'd they rope you, Coder?'

'They didn't. I came in to make a deal with Robles.'

Silk's eyes widened. 'What sort of a deal?'

'I can buy you out of here . . . that's if your father will come up with a thousand dollars.'

The prisoner turned his head and spat. 'Forget it, big man. I told you before, he hates my guts.'

'And I've told you that everything's changed. He's dying and wants to bury the hatchet with you before he goes.'

Confusion crossed Silk's features. 'Are you really on the level about that, bounty man?'

'I wouldn't be here if I wasn't. I'm next door to certain I can get you set loose, Silk, mainly because I've a powerful hunch Justin could and would come up with that money if he must. If you'd trusted me before instead of hightailing it when we crossed the big river we could have been back on the Silver Dollar by now.'

Silk's smile was more a smirk. 'So, the old man really wants to make up, eh? Well, I reckon that beats all.' Then he frowned. 'He know who and what I am

97

down here in *mañana* land?'

'No. And he's not going to know.'

'How's that?'

'I've gone through one hell of a lot to run you to ground, Silk. It's going to take a lot to get you out of this hell-hole and back home in one piece. But when we get there, you're not going to ruin everything. You are going to sit back and play the model son until Wardlaw cashes his chips. Compre? That would be the deal.'

'Judas! If I didn't know better, I'd almost reckon that me and the old man gettin' together again all nice and cosy was important to you, Coder.'

'It is.'

'Why?'

'You wouldn't understand. But we understand one another, don't we, outlaw? I'm sticking my neck out to try and save your life, so you'll play the game when you get home. If you don't, I swear that you and me will come to it and you'll wish to God you were back here facing the firing squad.'

Silk shook his head wonderingly.

'I'll be double-damned! Old Brown Man Coder's got his soft spot after all. Who'd have believed that one?'

'Cut the jaw, Silk. Have we got a deal or not?'

'Sure we have.'

Then Silk's handsome face turned cold.

'But none of this will play out, Coder. My old man and me hate one another's guts. There ain't no way known he will fork out serious money to pry me out of this pest hole. He might think he wants to see me before he croaks, but he don't want to see me one thousand dollars' worth.'

'You'd better pray he does,' Coder replied tersely, turning to the guards. 'All right, let's go.'

Kid Silk seemed so certain his father would fail to come up with the money for his release that uncertainty was niggling at Ryan Coder as he rode into the big Texas town of Sunrise City late the following afternoon.

It didn't take long for him to discover his error.

Immediately upon reaching Sunrise City he fired a wire off to Mission. He informed Wardlaw that his son Danny was alive and well but facing execution in a Mexican prison for a crime he didn't commit. The price of his release was set at one thousand American dollars.

The reply arrived at daybreak in the form of a wire instructing the First National Bank of Sunrise City to pay to Ryan Coder the sum of one thousand American dollars on demand. No questions, no hesitation, no demands for proof that Coder wanted the huge sum for the purposes he'd stated. There was just the wire to say the money was available, plus a touching message from the daughter: 'Our prayers for a safe return for both of you. Libby.'

The bank paid out the money without hesitation. Wardlaw had deposited one thousand dollars cash with the First National at Mission and the bank had already wired the Sunrise City branch to that effect.

By nightfall, Ryan Coder was again fording the Rio Grande at Pierro.

CHAPTER 7

FREEDOM ROAD

The tall walls of the *Rurale* station gleamed dull grey in the moonlight. It was two nights later and Coder was still waiting. Robles insisted the delay in releasing Kid Silk was due to 'strategic reasons', an explanation which told Coder nothing.

He'd seen Robles that afternoon and the captain had assured him the release would 'almost certainly' be effected tonight. Robles had sounded convincing but there was no way Coder could be sure. He didn't trust the man – which was the reason he'd paid only half the required cash so far and had seldom taken his hand off gunbutt in two days. If Robles was cooking up some kind of doublecross then Coder wouldn't be caught napping.

The moon cast the big gunfighter's shadow ahead of him as he paced the length of the station's north wall with his rifle in the crook of his arm.

101

He paused momentarily at the corner and was starting slowly back when he sighted the three *Rurale* riders coming up the trail from town.

He backed into deep shadow and stood watching. The trio clattered by making for the main gate. They appeared travel-weary and their mounts were lathered and blowing hard. He heard a gate guard challenge before the bunch passed from sight around the south-east corner.

He frowned and took out tobacco and papers. Although not a heavy smoker he'd been using plenty tobacco over these past days. He was at his best when things were moving. Inactivity and uncertainty always chafed him, made him edgy.

He'd just finished his smoke when he heard somebody at the north gate. The Winchester lifted as the gate swung open and the tall, slender figure of Robles appeared followed by the jaunty shape of Kid Silk.

'Coder?' Robles called.

He approached warily, rifle at the ready.

'There is no reason for mistrust, Coder,' Robles smiled as he reached them. 'As you see, I have produced your prisoner, safe and sound.'

'Howdy, Coder,' Silk greeted. 'Nice night for ridin', huh?'

'Could be,' Coder murmured. He moved to peer through the doorway into the courtyard. It was empty. He slowly lowered the rifle and turned back to Robles. 'No tricks,' he warned. 'Don't get the bright idea of sending men after us when we leave, for any reason. You'd find the cost of that way too high.'

'No tricks,' Robles assured. 'You have the balance of the money?'

Coder indicated the horse tethered to a tree a short ways off near the black he'd bought for Silk. 'In my saddle-bags.'

'Then you will get it for me?'

Coder drew his six-gun and flipped it to Silk. 'Watch him, Kid,' he said, and headed for the horses.

'A distrustful man, Mr Coder,' Robles sighed.

'Ain't he though?' grinned Kid Silk.

When Coder returned he was toting a fat paper-wrapped package. He handed it silently to Robles who ripped off the wrapping then fanned the thick wad of bills he found within. 'I shall not count it,' the man said. 'You have proven yourself a man to be trusted.'

'Then that's it,' Coder grunted. 'Let's make tracks, Kid.'

'Gentlemen,' Robles intoned. 'One *momernto*. There is something else.'

'Make it quick,' Coder growled. 'Something about you makes me edgy, mister.'

Captain Robles smiled forgivingly. 'I trust you, yet you do not trust me even though I have honoured my bargain to the letter. But perhaps what I have to report will leave you with a higher opinion of me?'

'Get on with it,' Kid Silk said, impatient now. 'I ain't the nervous kind but somehow I never feel all that flash hanging about a jailhouse, Robles.'

'Very well, I shall be brief. And what I must say is both brief and simple. Now that we have completed our transaction and you are free to go where you will, Silk, it is very important to me that you are not taken captive when you cross the line into Texas, as that could immediately cast suspicion upon myself.'

'Hell, we couldn't have that!' the Kid said with a sneer.

'This is no time for sarcasm,' Robles replied sharply. 'As I have said, I do not wish for you to fall foul of the law, for should this happen you might be 'persuaded' to reveal how it was you came to be set free. That could prove disasatrous for me personally. So it is in my interest that you reach Mission safely and with this in mind I have sent three of my scouts across the river under cover in order to ensure the way north to the Jimcrack Range is clear.' He looked directly at Coder. 'That, and that alone, was the reason for the delay, *señor*.'

'Go on,' Coder grunted.

'There is a company of Rangers stationed down-river,' Robles stated. 'Therefore I suggest you travel north by way of Big Bend Basin to reach the Jimcrack Divide – it's brutal country but it's the safest way to travel.' He spread his hands. 'Now, surely all this is more than enough to ensure that you leave here with a better opinion of me than you expected?'

Coder and Silk exchanged glances. Then Coder grunted, 'Is that all?'

The *Rurale* captain frowned. 'Yes.'

'Then we'll be seein' you. Come on, Silk.'

'See you when the grapes get ripe, Robles!' Kid Silk chuckled and followed Coder across to the horses.

The two mounted in silence with Robles watching pensively from the gate. Silk buckled on his saddle-bags which the *Rurales* had returned to him and they started down the long slope towards the river.

The moment they were out of earshot, Silk glanced back at the solitary figure in the gateway with a scowl.

'You swallow that stuff about the Rangers, big man?'

'They might just be around here someplace,' Coder replied.

'You figuring to go by the Basin, then?'

'No. I still don't trust him. We'll cut east of the Basin and go through the brush country to reach the Jimcracks. It will take longer but'll likely be safer.'

'Reckon I agree.'

Silk hipped around in his saddle to stare backtrail again. As he did, Coder leaned from his saddle and neatly plucked the six-gun from the man's belt. Eyes flaring in quick anger, the Kid snatched for the weapon but missed.

'What in hell did you do that for, Coder?'

'You crossed me once. I'm taking out insurance you don't try it again.'

'Damn your eyes! I could need that gun before we've gone a mile . . . maybe need it quick.'

'You'll get it if you need it. And your best chance of getting it quick is to stay close, like real close.'

Silk's eyes blazed viciously as they covered the next one hundred yards. But then abruptly the reckless smile reappeared and he seemed totally relaxed again as he fingered his hat back from his forehead.

'You're a real old woman, big man, but I suppose you're half-smart enough underneath. Guess that greasy son of a bitch Robles might have been right about you.'

'How's that?'

'When he said you don't trust nobody, nohow, noplace.'

'He was dead right,' Coder affirmed, leaning back in his saddle as they descended the steep bank to the river. 'And on account I trust you less than just about anybody, Kid, let me give you fair warning. I'd take you back dead instead of alive if you so much as look crosswise . . . you can believe that.'

The outlaw's laughter mingled with the rushing sounds of the Rio Grande. 'Me try and trick old wise and crafty Coder? I'd never be that dumb. Besides, I owe you. You just saved my life.'

'Just cut the gab and concentrate on getting across.'

'Whatever you say, big man. You're the boss.'

'Don't ever forget it.'

Rurale Corporal José Guardia crossed the courtyard to join Robles in the gateway. In the brilliant moonlight the tiny figures of two distant horsemen could be seen climbing the bluffs on the Texas side of the Rio Grande.

Robles took the long black cigarillo from between his teeth. 'How much?'

Guardia reached inside his tunic and extracted a wad of bills held together by a strip of rawhide.

'Seven hundred dollars, Captain.'

Robles blinked in astonishment. 'Seven hundred? I expected four hundred . . . perhaps five at most.'

'I believe it was all Benito possessed. He paid it willingly for our information on Silk.'

The captain shook his head, still bemused. Robles knew the *bandido* well. They were almost friends. Benito caused endless trouble along the Rio Grande with his rustling and killings, but because he paid Robles hefty sums of protection money on a regular basis the crooked captain was content to permit the desperado to roam and plunder virtually at will while he concentrated his attention on those outlaws not enterprising enough to pay him protection money.

Aware there was bitter blood between Benito and former henchman, Kid Silk, Robles had guessed the *bandido* leader might be willing to pay plenty to learn that Silk was planning to escape to the US – along with the route he would take.

So it had eventuated. He was virtually delivering Silk into Benito's hands, and from that point on it promised to be a far more relaxing life down here along the Rio without that baby-faced butcher around to raise hell. *Vaya con Dios*, Kid Silk! You had a good run but now it's over!

Robles broke a brief silence. 'Silk must have really cleaned Benito out this time for him to want him dead so badly.'

'A vast sum, I am told. Yet I think it is not so much the cheating with the *dinero* as the death of Benito's brother at Silk's hands that has him lusting for revenge.'

'Ah, yes, I had forgotten about that killing.' Robles was apt to overlook things like bloody murders in matters where big money was also involved. 'Benito was greatly attached to his young brother, I am told.'

'So it is said. It seems the brother, Manuel, discovered that Silk meant to deceive Benito and tried to stop him. . . .'

Guardia paused, squinting across the shimmering river. The Americans had vanished in the haze of distance. He licked his lips. 'They say Manuel caused the Kid some offence, and so he cut his heart out.'

'You are a great one for exaggeration, Guardia. Surely you simply mean he killed Benito's brother with a knife, no?'

'No, Captain. I mean the Kid ripped out the boy's heart then kicked it into a creek, such was his rage.'

Captain Robles licked dry lips and shook his head that such terrible things should be. And none of the many dead who haunted his own dark conscience would disturb his sleep this night, for Benito the Bloodthirsty would soon join the ghostly ranks of the dead – due to him.

His coffee had gone cold. Bligh Middleton realized he'd completely forgotten his drink after becoming

absorbed in the sheaf of reports which had accumu-
lated during his absence from his Cobby City office.
Thrusting the documents aside the Ranger officer
jangled the desk bell at his elbow to summon his
orderly.

Cable entered, brisk and efficient as always. 'Sir?'

'Another mug of coffee.'

'At once, sir.'

Middleton was still slumped in exactly the same
position as Cable had left him when the man
returned with a steaming pannikin of coal-black
coffee a short time later.

'You look beat, Captain,' the orderly observed.

'Feel it, too, Cable. Any word from the south?'

'Concerning Silk, sir?' the orderly asked and
Middleton nodded. Cable shook his head. 'Nothing,
sir. Were you expecting something?'

'Damned peculiar, these recent events. Last I
heard they were ready to execute him at Cracaw for
shooting a gambler. How come we haven't heard that
job's been done?'

'I think we both have learned to our cost that very
little about Silk is predictable, including news on him
either good or bad.'

'Why is it that I seem to be one of the few who sees
that baby-faced butchering young bastard for what
he is,' the lawman muttered, then broke off with a
sigh. He shook himself and looked up. 'And nothing
on Coder either, I suppose?'

'No, Captain. Do you still believe Coder had taken
Kid Silk prisoner and was maybe bringing him in for

the bounty money when you spotted them together along the Rio Grande that day?'

'That would make sense, at least. Oh, I know there's been gossip amongst the men that Coder and Silk might be in cahoots, but that seems impossible. I know Coder too well. As hard a man as any you'll ever meet and far too ready with a six-gun for my taste yet straight as a die in my book. And smart. He wouldn't be taken in by the Kid's charm like so many are—'

He broke off with a sigh.

'Well, that will be all for the moment, Cable. Just make sure you let me know right away if anything is heard on either Silk or Coder . . . and whatever the hell it is they are doing together.'

'Yes, sir,' the orderly said, and left.

Middleton sat unmoving and pensive for a long time, going over and over in his mind his recent campaign in the Big Bend region which had eventually resulted in the destruction of Kid Silk's old gang.

Finally he remembered his coffee. He lifted the cup to his lips, grimaced. It had gone cold again!

He was short and paunchy with a double chin and thick bowed legs. In his huge sombrero, rowel spurs and with double gunrig buckled tightly beneath sagging gut, Benito the *bandido* cut a slightly ridiculous figure – until you looked into his eyes.

There was nothing remotely odd or amusing about the Mexican killer's eyes. They were black and round with a fierce enamel shine. These were not the eyes of a jolly fat man but rather the chilling, spine-tingling orbs of a natural-born killer.

Benito the butcher had rarely appeared more menacing than that afternoon in Big Bend Basin as he stood listening to a report from his scouts who'd just returned from the river. The two had ridden downriver as far as Pierro, they revealed, and were back to report that, although they had not glimpsed Miguel Chavez in the flesh, they had cut two sets of strange tracks leading into the brush country.

Both scouts were hard-rock certain that one of the horses belonged to Kid Silk, so distinctive and flashy were those tracks.

Benito slammed a fist into a pudgy palm with a triumphant smack at this fresh news. Yet in the next breath he was bitterly castigating himself for not having realized Kid Silk would have far too much low animal cunning to blunder into the ambush he'd set for him!

The Kid and Benito hated one another with biblical intensity. And right now, Benito could envision all his many enemies sniggering to one another that once again the Kid had given him the slip and was likely laughing up his flash sleeve at him right at this very moment. Again!

The hellions waited patiently below as their leader strode back and forth punching his palm with hard leathery smacks of the fist. Then abruptly he propped and instead began banging his forehead with the heel of his hand and groaning, '*Stupido*!'

'Surely this poor brain is thick with stupidity!' He

accused himself. With a snarl he suddenly whirled about and came striding back along the rocky parapet gesticulating wildly at the men on the level below. 'The horses, *pronto*! *pronto*! We leave this accursed place at once!'

The men immediately began scurrying for the grassy rim where the horses were cached in thick timber. Benito's *segundo*, Miguel Abundio, thought it safe enough to hazard a fawning, expectant grin.

'You have the plan, *Caudillo*?'

'*Sí*. You recall when that stinking *Rurale* spy came to tell me of Silk's release? He spoke also at that time of the story the bounty hunter had told Robles.'

'You mean about Silk's father?'

'*Sí*. I paid little attention at the time, for I never knew the Kid had a father – or mother for that matter. And I sensed Guardia had little faith in the story himself. But now that I am at long last beginning to use my brain as it should be done, I think maybe perhaps it could be true.'

'I do not understand.'

'The money, fool. The *dinero*! We know the gringo Coder paid Robles much gold to buy the Kid's filthy life from the *Rurale*.' Benito spread his hands. 'There is right now a $5,000 bounty on the Kid's murdering head. Why would such a one as this Coder be willing to pay out even more than the Kid is worth to him unless he is taking him back to the north for some other reason besides bounty . . . perhaps for more bounty than any of us knows of. . . ?'

Abundio's eyes stretched wide. '*Caramba*! I think

maybe you strike upon the truth, Benito. Then you believe this Coder is indeed returning the Kid to his father, as he claims?'

'It can only be so.' Benito was brimming with excitement as he sensed so many puzzling things finally slotting into place. 'What was that place Guardia spoke of? Something with a name like a church. . . ?

'I think it was Mission.'

'Mission! *Sí*, that was it. How far is it to Mission, Abundio?'

'Many miles, *Caudillo*. Days of long riding . . . unless of course we were to take the short route through the Jimcracks?'

Eager faces turned suddenly sober. The Jimcrack Hills route offered the quickest and by far the shortest direct route from Mexico north through to Mission County. Yet few travellers ever attempted it, and with good reason. Nightmare country some called it, while others insisted that the violently twisting horse track-cum-trail through the tortured bowels of the hostile Jimcracks was to all intents and purposes no trail at all – unless for some reason you happened to be truly desperate to get north in record time.

Benito the Butcher had such a reason. It was called revenge against the most cunning and dangerous enemy he'd ever cultivated over years of slaughter and theft.

That enemy was Kid Silk, who had a year ago annihilated the Butcher's entire family in a fit of vengeful pique over a woman.

Within moments of the idea taking root in his brain, Benito the Butcher was making his plans, the most vital segment of which was time and speed.

Everything depended on the Butcher marshalling his band and riding day and night to reach the Jimcracks ahead of the man he hated more than death itself.

CHAPTER 8

DEAD MAN'S PASS

The doctor emerged from Justin Wardlaw's room and closed the door behind him. Libby turned from the window where she'd been watching the sun go down over the Silver Dollar. Doc Murphy was seventy with a reputation for grouchiness, yet the man could always manage a smile for Justin Wardlaw's daughter. In his opinion Libby Wardlaw was the best-looking woman in Mission County and he considered it a sad reflection on the young men of the county that she hadn't married years ago.

'How is Father, Doctor?' she asked.

'Hanging on, Miss Libby, just hanging on.'

'Is he better or worse than when you saw him last?'

'About the same.'

The physician set his black bag down on the small table by a bowl of flowers. He took a small black pipe from a waistcoat pocket and felt for his matches.

'You realize, of course, he's living on borrowed time, don't you, Libby?'

'Yes,' the girl replied gravely. 'I've known that for months.'

'And I guess you also know what's keeping him going?'

'The hope of seeing Danny before he dies.'

'Correct.' Murphy tamped shag-cut into the bowl of the pipe and studied the girl keenly. 'Do you reckon he's got good cause to hope that he'll see your brother again, Libby?'

'I-I'm just not sure, Doc. He told you of the message he received from Coder advising they were on their way, I suppose?'

'Uh-huh.'

Libby shrugged slim shoulders. 'I just don't know . . . simply don't know. I suppose it all comes down to whether Coder's word is to be trusted or not.'

'By the sound of that you don't trust him?'

'No, I don't.'

'Well, maybe it's not right for me to go building up false hope in your mind at a time like this, Libby, but I can't help feeling that if it's up to Coder then the chances of you seeing your brother might be a lot better than you think.'

She frowned.

'If I didn't know you better, Doc, I'd think I almost detected a note of admiration in your tone then. But surely I'm mistaken?'

Murphy moved to the window and locked his hands behind his back. Outside, the ranchland was

116

rose and gold in the twilight.

'I surely don't admire anybody who takes human life when my job is saving it, girl,' he said quietly. 'But I believe Coder's very different from most in his profession. You see, I patched him up a couple of years ago down at Cranebrook Falls after he was pretty badly shot up bringing in a couple of killers. Got to know him pretty well over a short space of time. Told me a lot about himself when he was feeling weak and puny that I reckon he'd never have told me otherwise. Like, for instance, how he doesn't see himself as the killer folks reckon he is, but just a man who does important jobs that nobody else has got either the guts or the gunspeed to take on.'

'It's a terrible profession.'

Murphy angled his head to study her keenly. 'Can't deny that, Libby. But there are lots of terrible people in this Texas of ours. If we didn't have men like Ryan Coder there'd surely be a whole heap more of the breed running around loose.'

'But surely he does that job simply for the money?'

'Maybe, maybe not.'

'I'm quite sure he only accepted the job father offered him for profit.'

'You could be wrong about that.'

'What do you mean?'

'Well, at first I was mighty surprised when I heard Coder had taken off in search of Danny, but when I got to reflecting on his rep and background I guess I got to thinking again.'

'How do you mean?'

117

'Well, again when Coder was sick that time in Cranebrook Falls he told me about his own father. Seems the old man ran off and left him and his ma destitute when he was just a tad. You could tell this was the worst thing ever happened to him and it seems he never did give up hope that the day would come when the father would return and they'd all be happy together again.'

'But he didn't come back?' she guessed.

'Nope. And you know it was kind of touching and sad to hear a big, hard fellow like Coder talking about his long-gone daddy that way. . . .'

'Well, I suppose that is sad enough, if true,' she conceded grudgingly. 'But I still don't see what it has to do with the present situation.'

'You don't?' Murphy collected his satchel and headed for the door. 'Well, mebbe I'm reading more into it than there is, Libby. Still, I still have this feeling that the main reason Coder agreed to search for your brother was on account he knows personally what it's like for a father and son to be parted – and you folks have been without your brother for a mighty long time.'

They stepped out on to the porch, Libby Wardlaw's expression thoughtful as she considered the other's words. But then she shook her head upon recalling the rocky-faced Coder she had met in Mission.

'An interesting notion, Doc, but I'm afraid, nothing more than that. It's simply not possible for me to see Coder as anything other than a man driven by

118

greed and a taste for killing.'

'Well, you could be right,' Murphy conceded, dumping his satchel in the back of his buggy. He untied the lines from the whip socket then studied the young woman squarely. 'But if I'm wrong about what motivated Coder to take on your assignment in the south, I know I'm right about one thing, at least. If he claims to have found your brother then you can believe it. And I also believe he'll bring him back home if that is humanly possible. I've never heard of Coder starting a job he didn't finish.'

Despite herself Libby couldn't suppress the quick leap of hope she experienced at that moment. For she desperately wanted to believe her father might get to see Danny again before he died. 'Thank you, Doc,' she said simply as he clambered up into the buggy. 'I needed a little encouragement today. Will we see you tomorrow?'

'Sure, Libby, I'll be coming by every day now until. . . .'

He broke off and forced a smile. 'What I mean is . . . I'll see you both tomorrow.' He slapped the lines. 'And keep your chin up, girl.'

She waved and Murphy gigged the pair of matched bays into a trot.

It was too bad about old Justin, Murphy reflected, as he swung out through the gates and went spanking along the town trail. But he at least could look back on a full life. It was Libby who worried him more. Operating an outfit the size of the Silver Dollar alone was no job for any girl to be left with as she would be in the near future.

Of course should Danny Wardlaw make it home at long last it might solve that problem . . . or maybe, it might make it worse?

He frowned.

What had he meant by that? He knew the answer only too well when he allowed his memory to slip back to that ugly day when he'd come out here three years ago to find Justin Wardlaw with the kid's bullet in his back and young Danny gone. . . .

He grimaced and gigged the horse into a swifter gait.

The faint wraith of the day's hoof-raised dust was fading away over the low ground below the campsite to mingle with the gloom of the gathering dusk. The sun was gone below the western rimrock leaving the sky awash with silver and crimson. The canyons along with the eastern face of the hills already lay in deep shadow.

Coder was shoving the coffee pot into the fire when an owl's hoot sounded from the shadowy gloom of the timberline. The big man swung his head sharply to listen to the strung-out notes of the night bird's cry, then turned back to his chore.

Sprawled out on the grass nearby with his saddle supporting his head, Kid Silk chuckled softly. 'You're jumpy, big man. Matter of fact you been jumpy ever since we put the Rio behind us, seems to me.'

Coder didn't reply. He was not nervous, merely alert. And he meant to stay that way. The boot hills of the West were filled with men who'd allowed weariness to get the better of them when travelling the wild trails.

Once he had the coffee pot bedded securely upon the glowing coals he rose and moved across to the small spring which burbled from the rocks close to where the horses were tethered. He hunkered down, facing Silk, then tugged the grubby bandaging from around his head and sluiced cold water over his healing wound. Exploring fingers told him the furrow had closed over. He wouldn't need the strapping now.

'You want me to take another look at that shoulder?' he asked.

'Hell, no. It's doin' just fine. I'm tough, Coder – all iron and rawhide.'

Coder returned to the fire and dropped the last of the bacon into the pan. The light was fading fast and stars began to wink overhead. He hunkered down on his spurs with elbows resting on his knees and big brown hands linked together. In the glow of flickering firelight his bronzed features were expressionless, only the eyes busy as he surveyed the shrouded landscape.

'So . . . how far now do you figure, Coder?' Kid Silk queried after a silence. 'It's so long since I was up this way I've forgotten most of the landmarks.'

'We're about halfway. Should get there two nights from now.'

Kid Silk stretched luxuriously and linked hands behind his head to gaze up at the stars. 'Only two nights to a happy family reunion,' he said with a crooked smile. 'I mean, it's plum touchin' just to think of the old man on his bed of pain waiting for the prodigal son to come across his doorstep before he croaks, surely is.'

'There are worse things can happen a man than being back home with his own kin,' Coder reminded. 'Didn't you ever come down with the urge to come visit home in those three years, Kid?'

'Never. I was havin' too fine a time.'

'Thieving and shooting folks, you mean?'

Silk propped himself up on one elbow. 'A man's gotta live, bounty man. Besides, I only ever did about one tenth of what they claim. I'd have had to be six wild men to pull all the capers they lay at my feet. You've been around, you know how these stories get started.'

Coder nodded. He knew only too well what it was like, for legend had it that he'd killed ten times more outlaws than was actually the case.

He still didn't know how much of the Kid Silk legend was fact and what pure fiction.

He knew the man to be both brave and dangerous, yet it was difficult to envision him as the bloody slaughterman he was reputed to be. Maybe Silk was more wild than vicious, and if that were so then it offered the hope that things might yet work out up north.

Maybe if the Kid could patch up things with his father it might be possible for him to settle down on the Silver Dollar. His crimes – fact or fiction – had been committed south of the border in the main. He might return to the anonymity of his given name, knuckle down and maybe. . . .

He shook his head and said, 'What would you do right now if I was to just ride off and leave you to make your own choice, Silk? Would you still go on home?'

'Sure,' came the ready reply. 'Hell, man, that old Silver Dollar can be worked up into a spread worth real *dinero*. And you know, if me and the old man make up, well, he's bound to leave me the place. It's sure for certain Libby couldn't handle it.'

'She's a fine girl, your sister.'

'Fine mebbe, but bossy.' The smile flashed. 'But there you go again, big man.'

'What?'

'You're getting that look in your eye whenever we mention my sister. You do it every time.' Silk sat up sharply, blue eyes twinkling. 'So, what's the score there anyway? You sweet on Libby?'

'Don't talk like a damn fool!'

'Hey, touched a nerve, huh?' He chuckled. 'Old Brown Man Coder soft on the Kid's sister . . . now there's a twist for you. But, hey . . . wouldn't it be something if you two got together, huh? We'd be one big happy family and we could sit around on the porch drinkin' from the jug and you and me yarnin' about all the fun and games we had down along the Rio Grande.'

Annoyance worked in Coder as he rose quickly and went across to check on the horses.

He was riled because it was true. Libby Wardlaw occupied his mind far more than she should. And there were times when he got to thinking about her that he began having crazy thoughts, like hanging up the guns and settling down.

And that was just plain foolish. For that girl plainly despised who and what he was, he knew. Libby Wardlaw regarded him as a killer and maybe she was right. But at least he was going to prove her wrong in one respect, he reassured himself. She had told him in Mission she expected him to bring her brother home dead. He wondered if she mightn't change her mind and think better of him when he finally rode in with Danny alive and well at his side.

The food was ready when he returned to the fire.

In silence he broke out plates and cutlery. The Kid was studying a piece of thick paper, and grinning. Curious, Coder moved around behind him to see that the slip was a Mexican wanted dodger. It featured an excellent likeness of the Kid and stated in bold print that down in Old Mexico the *Americano bandido* and killer known as Kid Silk was worth five thousand pesos, dead or alive.

'Where'd you come by that?' he demanded.

'I had it tucked away in my saddle-bags.'

'You'd better get rid of it then.'

'No chance.'

Coder reached for the dodger but Silk thrust it inside his shirt then pushed his hand away. 'I'm hangin' on to this one, Coder. If I settle down like I plan and end up fat and fifty one day, I could haul this thing out and get to relive the good old days.'

Coder loomed above him. 'I want that thing, Silk. If it fell into the wrong hands—'

'Don't crowd your luck, Coder,' Silk said quietly. 'I've gone along with you because it suited me . . . so far. But just don't push me, big man. The Kid hates bein' crowded.'

'You talk like it's you that's got the gun and weigh fifty pounds heavier than me, outlaw. I could take that thing off you easy if I really wanted.'

'Mebbe you could do that . . . but it wouldn't be easy, Coder. And even if you did, I'd get it back and you could end up dead . . . if you really got me sore. . . .'

Coder was peeved yet impressed. For he knew the Kid had courage and ability to burn – there could be no mistake about that. Maybe he could take the dodger by force but he didn't consider it that important. He felt they had built up some sort of wary rapport on the trail and didn't want to risk that at this late stage.

'All right,' he grunted, moving back to the fire. 'But I still say hanging on to something like that is just plain dumb and a big risk.'

'Haven't you heard, big man?' the other grinned, forking a slab of meat. 'I been livin' risky all my life.'

The *bandidos* rode north at speed.

They were strangers here but Miguel Abundio's trailsmanship and sense of direction kept them dead on course as surely as if he'd had a compass set in the swell-fork pommel of his Spanish-Texas saddle.

The terrain slowly changed character as they left the plains country behind. Here was a landscape of brushy, hog-backed ridges, rock-bench slopes and deep canyons. Occasionally they passed through tight little valleys dotted with piñons and gnarled old oaks. Willows, cottonwoods and junipers marked the watercourses.

The third morning of their journey from Big Bend Basin started out cloudy and overcast but the sun forced its way through while they nooned in a wooded canyon. It blazed strongly throughout the afternoon.

The riders were growing weary and the further they pushed north-east the more rugged the country, but they didn't gripe about that. Even the newest recruit was aware that the fat little man in the huge sombrero riding lead was in no mood to listen to any complaints this time out.

It was common knowledge Kid Silk had cheated Benito and slain his brother in the most brutal fashion and Benito had sworn bloody revenge. Now it was the bunch's duty to help the boss achieve his goal.

They comforted themselves with the thought that when Kid Silk breathed his last – maybe just days or even hours ahead now – that lethal look would finally leave Benito's face and he would once again be the old laughing *compañero*-cum-leader they remembered. Then it would be straight back home to the Rio Grande where they belonged to kick the dirt of this hostile landscape off their boots for keeps.

Towards evening the land opened out, spreading into wide, rolling shelves of grassland. The breeze picked up, refreshing weary horses. They rode through huge stands of cottonwoods, splashed across a little stream, then started up a long brown slope as the yellow sun sunk towards the western rim.

Upon topping out the crest Benito raised a hand to bring them to a halt. There was satisfaction in the stocky leader's face as he gestured north at the steep line of broken-backed mountains stretched across the skyline. It had been years since Abundio had been this far north yet his trailsmanship had brought them unerringly here.

'The Jimcrack Hills . . . ugliest range in the country!' Benito announced over the sounds of jingling harness and blowing horses. 'Only one way through, and, let me warn you, *amigos,* this is a very difficult trail through Heartbreak Pass. But I have been through there before so it shall soon be behind us.'

He paused, the cruel and pudgy face taking on a glow of real animation. 'And beyond the barricade lies Mission County.'

They watched their leader warily as he took out a spotted bandanna and swabbed his sweating face. His odd mood this journey scared them just a little even if they were his loyal *compañeros*. It didn't make them feel any more relaxed when he was heard muttering to himself: 'Soon we shall see if he can die as bravely as he kills,' and knew he was obsessing about the Kid.

They rested briefly, listening to the innocent sounds of horned larks and longspurs, the wild, plaintive notes coming from no apparent direction.

Then Benito gave the signal and they kicked on refreshed for the stony barricade of the Jimcrack Hills and were soon making their way for Heartbreak Pass . . . swarthy, alien horsemen outlined against the crimson backwash of the sun with only murder on their mind.

CHAPTER 9

TO KILL THE KID

Kid Silk had been singing on and off ever since he awoke. As the moon came up he launched into a new tune while Coder saddled the horses deep within the titanic stone cavern nature had gouged out over the centuries deep down in the Jimcrack Hills.

The way of a cowboy, so happy so free,
No women, no corrals . . . no siree,
Free to get drunk, free to just lie,
Free if you like, to lay down and die.

He broke off laughing. 'You like that one, big man?'

'I've heard better.'

'The next verse is just as good. You listen. . . .'

The next verse proved far worse but Coder didn't even hear it as he stood surveying the intimidating

129

reality of Heartbreak Pass just a rifle shot ahead now.

He was every bit as alert today as he'd been when crossing the Rio Grande days earlier, his gaze intently playing over that fantastic tumble of quake-stricken hills, canyons and massive overhangs which loomed forbiddingly before them. Nightmare country, but still the quickest and shortest way north to more peaceful country for men who might have reason to fear pursuit.

He uncapped his water canteen and took a sparing sip. It could always be a nightmare journey through the myriad twists and convolutions of the dangerous canyon pass but once that was behind them, the good grasslands and open spaces of Mission County lay ahead.

He felt refreshed yet still intended grabbing a couple hours' rest before tackling the challenge of Heartbreak Pass. There were a dozen entryways into the Jimcracks from the south but all finally chan-nelled down into the one twisted tunnel through to the north known as the Heartbreaker.

A two-hour rest had him feeling ready for anything by the time they'd completed their saddling, then swung up again to make their wary way through a subterranean world – the rockslides, chasms and moonlight and shadows leading onwards into the strangeness and muted echoes of the mountain's interior.

They passed a rock formation resembling a howl-ing gargoyle that was eerily half swallowed by deep pools of moonshadow. Kid Silk's lousy singing echoed jarringly from gaunt walls and and cliff faces. Steel-shod hoofs rang sharply on stone and a hunting owl beat its way overhead as they entered the exit tunnel proper, and Coder calculated they'd put a half-mile behind them – when it happened.

A night bird overtook them to disappear into the lofty patchwork of shadowy pits of gloom and contrasting moonwashed slabs of talus stone ahead. A short time later, with walls now closing in on all sides, the bird reappeared to shoot back the way it had come with a sharp cluck of alarm and flashed from sight.

Coder felt uneasy as he scanned his surrounds because something had plainly scared it away from its flight to the northern exit, which was their own objective.

Deep in a stony recess ahead his gaze caught a glimpse of furtive movement then heard an unfamiliar voice ring out.

'Silk!'

His hissed whisper cut through the outlaw's singing as the party reined in stirrup to stirrup. Coder palmed his spare Colt from holster and flipped it to an astonished Kid Silk without taking his gaze from that suspect spot dead ahead. He was aware they'd reined up in a brilliant bar of revealing moonlight, and his mind raced like a triphammer.

Cut back the way they'd come or dismount here and take to the shadows? For the one thing certain was that something had startled that fool bird and just maybe it had been something human.

'Into the rocks!' he shouted, and dived from the saddle clutching his rifle.

Hidden guns opened up thunderously as the two sprinted for the shadows with bullets spanging viciously off stone and their horses clattering away, trailing their lines.

A bullet smacked the floor of the pass close to Coder's boots and a flying chip of stone slashed his kneecap. He dived headlong behind a boulder, whipped Winchester to shoulder and loosed a volley of fire at the gunflashes flaring above. Somewhere close by in the enveloping darkness, Kid Silk's revolver emitted a reassuring roar.

Moments later a jagged scream sliced through the snarl of gunfire and a dark figure from up above came plummeting down with arms and legs flailing, screaming all the way down until he slammed into the floor with a dead meat thud to lie lifeless in in a square of moonlight.

'That there is Salazaar!' The Kid sounded astonished. 'That son of a bitch rides with Benito, big man!'

Coder bobbed low as bullets came whistling through moonlight and shadow to strike the crown of the boulder inches from his shoulder.

Benito!

This was hard to believe for he figured he'd given that bunch the slip a long way back. He wanted to believe Salazaar's moonwashed corpse was not proof Benito had second-guessed them and broke all records to get here ahead of them, yet instantly knew it had to be so.

Ambush guns were storming from all over right now and yet he was calm and he concentrated coolly as he rested his rifle upon a rock and cut loose with a volley that angled upwards to pepper a high yellow rock shelf where two enemy guns were now spitting flame.

Moments later a second ambusher was struck and plummeted a hundred feet to his doom . . . and Silk's weapon beat heavy thunder as it followed him down.

'It's only Benito and his bunch of losers, big man!' the Kid cried excitedly. 'Here, gimme another gun and we'll charge the bastards!'

Coder flipped the .45 across but didn't shift position one inch. 'Charge? Up there? You out of your mind?'

'It's just tenth-rate scum, damnit.' Silk bobbed up to snap off a quick shot, dropped flat again. 'I know this greaser breed. I can tell you there ain't one of them up to our class, not even fat old Benito himself. So let's roll right over 'em while we got a full head of steam and they are rattled.'

His bravado forced Coder to reconsider.

It was plain they'd held their own thus far yet the odds against remained high and should the Mexes get smart and start working down closer to them from opposite sides of their nest of rocks their position down here could quickly turn into a death trap.

Retreat would be suicidal, which only left . . . what? The Kid's course?

'All right.' He heard his own voice echoing as if

coming out of a tomb as he squinted through the roiling clouds of gunsmoke now fogging the pass. 'Let's do it!'

But on the instant a volley of orange-red gunflame from above caused the pair to drop belly flat and vicious shot spattered about them. This was followed by the bellowing discharge of a heavy rifle that struck rock above them to shower their tucked-in heads with rock chips and drifting dust.

A man appeared howling and the Kid pumped four bullets into the buckling body when one would likely have done.

The odds were evening out – but for how much longer?

Both men rolled from sight while the enemy reloaded with feverish haste, the ensuing dog fight stretching into deafening minutes with no further casualties. It appeared as though the second-raters amongst the enemy had been culled early leaving only top guns to shoot it out in the giant echo chamber that was Heartbreak Pass.

But the Texans maintained the strategic advantage and used it to the full when a Mexican suddenly leapt up with rifle at the shoulder – only to have Silk cut loose with gunflame spurting from both hands.

The riddled killer tumbled and was still falling as Coder's big frame went driving upwards past the Kid's position. Both men cut loose at a blur of movement off to their left. A rifle clattered down, a reeling figure lurched into a bar of blinding moonlight to be instantly blown backwards off his feet by their combined volley – and those gringo guns did roar!

A rifle clattered down followed closely by an arms-flailing figure who'd missed his footing to fall thirty feet, screaming all the way down.

Kid Silk ducked fast but not quite fast enough. The plummeting figure struck him hard and Coder cursed as both figures tumbled and vanished into the yawning black moonshadow beneath.

He glanced upwards to see a face barely feet from his own – a snarling Mexican face with eyes glittering and teeth bared in an animal snarl.

The two triggered together and Coder ducked aside only just in time as the corpse with staring eyes and a hole in the forehead went plunging past, raging no longer.

Coder heard the dead man thud as the body struck the pass floor far below, then nothing. He waited, realizng only now he was sweating like a plough mule with his heart going like a trip-hammer. He was waiting for the next shot, the next voice.

But suddenly there was only gunsmoke and silence.

'Hey – Kid!'

No response. But moments later a Mexican rifle bellowed from somewhere up high to be quickly answered by the roar of an American Colt .45.

This told him the Kid was still alive but deeper within the pass now.

Coder headed in that direction, leaping from rock to rock, reloading as he went. His lungs burnt and his chest ached yet he drove himself to geater effort as gunfire exploded again and he now glimpsed the shimmer of gunflashes flickering higher up against the opposite wall.

He reached ground level but it was only to realize that the sheer uproar of the guns prevented him from getting a bearing on where the action was centred.

So he was forced to hunker down and wait for what seemed an eternity before running feet sounded close by and he whirled to glimpse a big-hatted silhouette charging by.

He fired. The *bandido* somersaulted, smacked head-first into a pillar of solid stone and slumped to ground, leaving Coder free to go hunting again. Even if Silk had fought with rare courage, the man was still his prisoner and he must run him down regardless of the risk.

Twenty exhausting minutes later found him still combing the eerily echoing higher inner spaces of Heartbreak Pass. He was climbing towards the gunflashes, a big man breathing hard and labouring, losing balance. . . .

He fell again.

He knew he'd been out cold for some time when he sat up sharply. He turned his head warily, realizing he lay just where he had fallen. No menacing figures in big hats, no storming guns . . . just that hideous sound of someone screaming in terrible agony. . . .

He rolled on to his chest, grimacing. He'd fallen hard but hadn't broken anything, and flexing power-ful arms he knew he could still fight if he must.

Back on his feet he staggered across to a dead bandido and relieved him his pistol. That formless, shrieking was now quite close, he realized. Then he heard another sound blending with it. Wild laughter . . . strangely familiar. . . .

In the end it seemed only by chance that he finally stumbled upon a scene he would never forget . . . and immediately glimpsed the Kid.

Silk knelt upon a rock ledge with his back to him some fifty feet distant and his hysterical laughter was that of a madman. . . .

The Kid moved and Coder sighted the second man . . . leastwise he reckoned it was a man. He felt his blood chill as his gaze riveted upon the blood-drenched figure of a burly Mexican whose red shirt alone identified Benito and from him those hideous sounds continued to bubble from a tongueless mouth.

He stared disbelievingly.

Benito's ears were gone . . . there were empty sockets where his eyes had been . . . the bulging belly had been slit open neck to crotch . . . disembowelling him. The victim was still alive but barely, his pudgy hands fluttering helplessly upon the crimsoned rock floor like dying fish. He was the butchered centrepiece in a sea of blood.

The blade in Kid Silk's hand slashed swiftly again as he cried gleefully, 'Aiiee, Benito, can you still hear me, *compañero?*'

Coder didn't move, could not drag his eyes from the hideous scene as in that one searing moment he realized the Kid was not as bad as some painted him – but was frighteningly and inhumanly worse . . . unfit to live. . . .

He finally found his voice. 'Silk!'

The crouched figure leapt and whirled like a wild mountain cat to face him, wide-eyed and staring, with a gun in one hand and a dripping blade in the other. Their eyes locked across twenty feet and then the Kid's gun was sweeping towards him faster than seemed possible – and yet in that moment of total desperation Coder proved the swifter. . . .

His gun exploded with a cannon's roar and the yellow banner of Kid Silk's hair instantly turned crimson as he crashed lifeless across the body of the enemy he'd so grotesquely butchered.

Coder knew he was dead before he struck stone yet could not hold back the second and third shots he drilled into the corpse with brutal concussions of sound.

Soon all seemed deathly quiet in Breakneck Pass.

For some reason Libby Wardlaw had trouble sleeping that night. She would drift off and doze lightly for a time then awaken, conscious of an acute sensation of dread.

And yet she was actually sleeping in that deep and final hour of the night and felt peaceful and relieved to awaken at last to see the pearly grey light of approaching dawn.

She arose and dressed quickly then spent several minutes brushing her hair before stepping out on to the gallery. The feeling of horror and foreboding which had haunted her whole night gradually faded as she stood gazing out over the familiar landscape.

Early morning was her favourite time of day on Silver Dollar. In this grey hour following first light and before the coming of the sun, the ranch buildings and the acres beyond appeared to drift silently in a gentle silvery haze.

Then the glow of the stable light faded and the dust of the yard changed slowly from grey to pale yellow.

Nobody abroad yet. This was the rare time when headquarters was devoid of noise or the bustle of activity. This was the time for ranch cats to prowl and forage before the early rising dogs appeared to chase them off.

Soon coyotes began singing from the distant hills and, as if it were a signal, Stan Dixon, the ranch cook, emerged from his hut next to the cookhouse to raise the familiar clatter of pots and pans that roused the sleepers in the bunkhouse nearby.

By the time smoke tendrils rose from the cookhouse chimney ranch hands were emerging, hawking, putting on their hats and squinting up at the sky to see what kind of day it would be.

Then the light was rapidly strengthening and Libby returned inside to see if her father was awake. She found him sitting up in bed and he greeted her with a weary smile.

'Up and about early today, Libby.'

'I didn't sleep too well, Father,' she said, adjusting

the pillows behind his back. 'But you did, didn't you?'

'I suppose so. . . .'

'Only suppose? But I looked in on you and you were sleeping soundly.'

'Oh, I slept all right. But I had dreams, Libby . . . bad dreams.'

'What kind were they?' she asked, plumping his pillows.

'I can't clearly recall now. But whatever was happening, it was something evil and wrong.'

She studied his face intently at this, for she'd had exactly that same sensation during the night and it had prevented her sleeping. Coincidence? Of course, she assured herself, practical and down to earth as usual. Then she said briskly, 'I'll go down and fix you some coffee, Father.'

'Thanks, honey. How many days is it now?'

She paused in the doorway. She knew what he meant. 'Since we heard from Coder, you mean?'

'Yeah.'

'Six days today, Father.'

'Seems a long time not to hear anything.'

'Now don't start fretting about that. They'll come.' She was smiling as she went out. 'Coffee won't be long.'

She went through to the kitchen and put a match to the kindling wood she'd set in the stove. Helen, the house cook on the ranch, hadn't appeared yet. Libby took down the coffee can and was spooning grounds into the pot when she heard a shout from the yard. Setting can and pot aside she went to the window and looked out. Ranch foreman Sherwood and two of the hands were standing in front of the tack-room gazing towards the south graze. Tommy Childs pointed and called something to the older man. She thought she caught the word, 'Coder!'

Her hands flew to her stomach to quell the sudden excitement. She ran down the corridor and out into the yard. Her steps slowed the moment Brad Sherwood turned sharply and looked at her. The ramrod's face was pale and tight-lipped. She stared past him to see hands running towards the title gate.

Moments later she sighted the big rider coming in past the old oak beyond the cattle troughs. He was dressed in brown and she would have recognized his heavy, wide-shouldered figure anyplace. Coder was leading a second horse, and for a moment the girl thought the saddle of that animal was empty. Then, as Coder turned to come round the troughs, she saw the body bag strapped across the saddle.

'Danny!' The cry broke from her lips and Brad Sherwood made to reach for her. But she brushed him aside and rushed for the gate, hair streaming in the sunlight.

The tired horses plodded slowly through the gateway. As always, Coder appeared tall and impressive astride that big paint stallion yet beneath his hat the powerful face was noticeably strained and pale and he was leaning a little to one side in the saddle. His gaze fixed upon the girl's face as she halted twenty feet away.

141

It was with terrible effort that Libby forced herself forward to finger back the canvas flap covering the face of the body slung across the horse behind the big rider.

Coder watched the shock hit her. The dead man's eyes were closed. There was a bullet wound to the side of his head.

She raised her eyes from the lifeless body to meet the horseman's bleak stare.

'So, you brought my brother home just as I said you would, Mr Coder. Dead!'

'I'm sorry.' Coder's voice was unsteady and there was hell in his eyes.

CHAPTER 10

SANCTUARY

The reunion between Justin Wardlaw and his long-lost son was a moment Coder had pictured in his mind many times since quitting Mission, seemingly an age ago now. Yet the drama of the actual event drove everything else from his mind but what was taking place in this room.

Often on manhunts Coder had promised himself that one day a job might wind up happily. Once or twice recently he'd tried to convince himself that this miracle could possibly happen with the Wardlaws. How crazy was that? All there was here was harrowing, brutal reality.

Leaning against the wall of the room where they'd laid out Kid Silk's body the manhunter watched bleakly as the old man, who'd aged years in mere weeks, finally turned away from the body to lean heavily upon his daughter's arm. Then Wardlaw propped, staring at him.

'Are you still here, Coder? I thought you'd have gone to get that wound attended to, man. Libby, see to it that Coder takes it easy and—'

'There's time enough for that later,' Coder said. 'First, I want to tell you how it happened. That's more important at the moment.'

Wardlaw made to protest but Coder overrode him as he led the way through the house to the big front room. As Wardlaw and Libby came through behind him, the girl said quietly:

'You might as well know that no matter what story you tell us, Mr Coder, I will never believe other than that you were responsible for my brother's death!'

'Please, Libby,' the old man objected with just a hint of his former authority. 'I'm not sure you're being quite fair to Coder.' He turned back to the bounty man. 'Please go ahead, we're listening.'

Coder leaned back against the wall. He didn't care to sit for fear he might not be able to make it back on to his feet. The weakness seemed to be intensifying, but what he wanted to tell the Wardlaws simply could not wait.

'Your son's death was my fault, Wardlaw,' he began. 'I want that made plain from the start.' He nodded at the girl. 'I guess you won't have much trouble believing that, miss?'

'Your fault?' Wardlaw said. 'How come?'

'Never mind . . . let's go back a ways so you'll know it all . . . I found Danny working as a ranch foreman on a spread down by the Rio Grande. He'd been there most of those three years he was away and those good folks reckoned him about the finest young fellow they'd ever met.'

He paused, watching the light come back to the old man's eyes. He went on.

'Danny was leery about coming back home, at first. It wasn't that he didn't want to – he surely did. All the old troubles were over and forgotten as far as he was concerned. Yet he found it hard to believe that you really wanted him back and I had to spend a couple of days convincing him of that.'

'But he finally did agree to return?' Wardlaw prompted after a silence.

'Yeah. And it was the day we were leaving that things first began to go wrong. You see, there was this Mex outlaw named Benito who had some old scores to settle with me from the past. We crossed trails with Benito's bunch and there was hell to pay. They chased us clear across the Rio, I gunned down a couple of Benito's men, and next thing the *Rurales* were on top of us.

He paused to glance from the window; he had to get his story straight, make it credible.

'I got away but they grabbed Danny. He would've been a goner if I hadn't got a tip that the *Rurales* captain could be bought off. Thanks to that money you wired down, I bought Danny's freedom and it looked like plain sailing for home. And that's how it proved to be . . . until we reached the Jimcracks.'

Coder paused to suck in a deep breath.

'Benito was laying for us at the Jimcracks. He must

have figured where we were headed and got there ahead of us.'

He broke off, staring at the windows. They appeared blurred with a crimson light, like blood. He shook his head, licked dry lips and continued.

'There was a bunch of them. They jumped us without warning. I was wounded early. They would have finished me then and and there but for Danny. He fought them off single-handed. He stood those hellions off until I could chime in again and between us, side-by-side, we whipped them good. There was only one of them still standing when Danny got hit. He didn't die right off. He lasted long enough to say I was just to tell you that all that happened long ago was all his fault, and that . . . and that he loved you.'

It was silent in the big room for a long time. Coder could not see the old man's face clearly yet caught the glimmer of tears in his eyes when he finally raised his head.

'He-he was always a good boy,' the rancher said slowly. 'Yet for some reason I always feared he might turn out badly with that hot temper of his. Yet hearing what sort of man he'd become now somehow takes the pain out of his dying . . almost. . . .'

'He was a son to be proud of,' Coder stated firmly. He glanced at the girl as he pushed his weary bulk off the wall, and her face appeared puzzled somehow. But that wasn't important right now. What was vital was that he get the hell out of here while he could still walk.

'Mr Coder!' Wardlaw called after him as he started

across the room. 'In spite of the fact that my son is now dead I still consider you earned your fee. You have the balance of one thousand dollars coming to you.'

'Father!' the girl remonstrated, and her voice seemed to echo in Coder's throbbing head. She said something further but he didn't hear. Suddenly the room spun crazily, he grabbed wildly at a bureau, then spun into darkness.

Doc Murphy shook his grey head wonderingly as he took Coder's pulse. 'Constitution of a horse,' he muttered.

'Does that mean I'm fit enough to ride?' the patient growled.

'All it means is that you are pickin' up,' Murphy stated. 'Mebbe you'll be able to starting thinking about horsebacking in five or six days – maybe.'

Coder scowled from his pillow as the medico collected his gear and packed it away into his satchel. He lay propped up against three fat pillows in the big four-poster in the Silver Dollar's airy front room. He was stripped to the waist and his barrel chest was encased in strapping. Three days earlier Murphy had prised a slug out of his rib-box, informing him that the bullet he'd taken in the Jimcracks had missed a vital organ only 'by a whisker'.

For the next two days Coder was too played out to do anything but just rest while Libby Wardlaw attended him. But he'd finally coaxed some strength back into his muscles just this third morning, and with it had come the restlessness. Maybe he wasn't fit enough to sit a saddle just today, but tomorrow would be a different story. No chance he would still be in this bed come tomorrow.

As if sensing how his patient's thoughts were running, the old medico returned to the bedside and jabbed a gnarled finger at his face.

'A week's rest at the inside, Coder!'

'How long since you spent a week on your back, old man?'

'I don't trail about shootin' up the countryside and be gettin' shot up in return, sonny!' Murphy snapped his satchel shut with an air of finality. 'One week!' he repeated, and stamped out.

The morning passed slowly.

Libby looked in on him several times, cool and impersonal as always. Coder realized he owed much of his recovery to the girl yet sensed she would have paid the same attention to a range bull with a busted leg – caring yet uninvolved.

Wardlaw came in around noon and the two men yarned quietly for a half-hour until Coder felt himself growing drowsy. When he awoke it was mid-afternoon and Libby was standing by the bed.

'How do you feel now?' she asked.

'Mending.'

'Do you feel well enough to receive a visitor?'

He pushed up on his pillows. 'Depends on who it is.'

'It's a Texas Ranger by the name of Middleton. He wants to ask you some questions about that gunfight in the Jimcracks.'

The following hour was testing. Middleton had set out for Mission immediately upon hearing news of the murderous battle with the Benito gang. The Ranger didn't attempt to hide his satisfaction that Benito was dead but it wasn't the outlaw who interested the captain most today. It soon became apparent he mainly wished to discuss Danny Wardlaw.

The conversation was still young when Coder first sensed the lawman had deep suspicions about Danny Wardlaw's true identity. Over time he heard how the lawman had flushed killer Kid Silk from the Big Bend Basin and how Benito and his bunch had tailed them across the Rio Grande. It had only been during that lengthy pursuit that it had belatedly dawned upon the peace officer that Silk and Wardlaw were of the exact same age, colouring and build. This had first aroused suspicion which had blossomed into almost certainty in the man's mind by now as he fixed Coder with his hard lawman's stare and asked the big question: 'Were those two hellraisers actually one and the the same?' he demanded.

Coder continued to lie until the lawman threatened to exhume Danny Wardlaw's body. Only then did Coder realize he had no option; there was no way out. So he spilled the truth but exhorted the lawman to say nothing to the Wardlaws. 'It wouldn't achieve anything for them to know how their son and brother turned out, Middleton,' he reasoned. 'Look, you've got what you came to find out, man. Close the file on him and just let him lie.'

Middleton was not unmoved by his plea, yet he refused to give Coder the assurance he demanded before quitting. When Libby visited some time later, hoever, it was to inform him that the Ranger had quit for Cobb City without any further mention of Kid Silk. Curious. . . .

Coder finally slumped back on his pillows, exhausted. Middleton still hadn't given him an answer. A good man, Bligh Middleton, he remembered thinking. He slept without dreaming.

It was around ten that night when Libby Wardlaw eventually braced herself for the chore she had been dreading for days. Seated at the lamplit table in her bedroom she unbuckled her brother's saddlebags and forced herself to go through his effects.

She'd thought she'd cried all her tears, but her eyes quickly grew misty again as she drew out a gaudy red shirt, a box of revolver bullets and a girl's pretty kerchief which still carried a lingering fragrance.

How little she had known her brother, she realized. For even when he had been living here, sharing the same house, Danny had always been a stranger. She had loved him yet feared the wild explosiveness of his nature. The siblings had been at once both close and remote. Now he was gone, leaving behind nothing more than memories and a handful of sad possessions.

There were odds and ends rammed down into the bottom of the first saddle-bag; an old watch, the firing pin from a Colt repeater; a dog-eared book about horses. Carefully setting the items to one side she drew the second satchel across the table and began to empty it. She thought she'd completed the task when she glimpsed the corner of a poster peeping from what was obviously some kind of secret compartment carefully stitched into one side of the satchel. She took hold of the the poster, drew it out and unfolded it upon the table.

Her brother's face, smiling and reckless, looked back at her from beneath a cocky black sombrero above the bold black letters which read, 'WANTED: KID SILK'.

At first her numbed brain refused to accept that what she was looking at was a Ranger's reward dodger identifying her brother as Kid Silk – wanted right across northern New Mexico for murder and cattle rustling.

Ashen-faced, disbelieving, she drew back from the poster. This had to be a mistake. Ryan Coder had said. . . .

Coder!

Suddenly she was on her feet and rushing from the room. She burst through the patient's door but halted on realizing he was sound asleep. Should she awaken him? She moved slowly across the room to stand by the bedside. By the glow of the turned-down lamp the big gunman's face appeared peaceful, almost boyish. The dodger in her hand trembled as she raised it and studied it again.

This couldn't be true!

Why would Coder lie?

What was the real truth about Danny?

Coder stirred and she backed away. She could wait until morning. But back in her room staring down at the picture she knew she was only delaying the inevitable. For with that first brutal jolt of shock receding, Libby Wardlaw at long last found herself – for the very first time in her life – finally coming to recognize the great single secret of her life. And that was that deep down she had always half-suspected what that brutal Wanted dodger trumpeted so loudly – namely that the brother she'd loved had in truth been a killer and outlaw.

And finally conceded for the first time in her life, remembering all those small cruelties and mad rages of her brother's childhood, that she'd always known Danny had been born under a dark star. . . .

The stallion had been rested and fed on good oats for four days and naturally was feeling frisky and ready to fight. The animal took its fist nip at him when Coder entered the stables and its half-hearted snap actually grazed his elbow. The man retaliated with a punch to the snout and yet the blow lacked either conviction or authority.

'No time for foolishness this morning,' Coder muttered, struggling to slip on the head harness. He spoke quietly. Daylight was still but a grey streak on the horizon and the Silver Dollar lay asleep all around. Coder felt rubber-legged and puny in comparison with his customary robustness, but still knew he could make it to Mission. They had fine rooms at the Frontier Hotel. He would spell up there for a few days more, drink plenty whiskey and get himself ready for the next job.

The next job! He grimaced and shook his head. Old habits died hard, he realized. 'The next job', meaning gun job, was a meaningless phrase to him now. For it was back during his bouts of delirium that he'd realized with startling finality that for Ryan Coder there could never be another gun job, another manhunt, another slaughterhouse like Heartbreak Pass. . . .

But now he found reality staring him in the face. If not the gun trails – then what? For the Kid's death hadn't really changed anything. He still loved the sister – she still despised him. Which left two options. He could stay and grovel to her before he was finally thrown out . . . or he could keep his dignity and simply fork leather and keep riding until he was back in Reality County . . . a man with a gun he could never use again.

He was lost in thought as he hauled his saddle down off the tree and dumped it on to the paint's back. But for a rare time his imagination came up empty. The future for men like him never altered, he brooded . . . a future of violence and dead men . . . of emptiness and loneliness with nothing to look forward to but survival . . . until the day came when you no longer cared if you survived or. . . .

The horse was making saddling difficult, slewing away and attempting to catch him with its big swinging head. Sweat erupted on Coder's brow. He rested briefly against the stall wall then mustered his strength to deliver a solid kick. The animal reared but made no further attempt to fight with the result that the saddling was quickly completed . . . just as the first curious beam of sunlight winked over the hills.

The light strengthened rapidly as Coder led the big paint past the darkened house. He stopped abruptly. Libby Wardlaw stood in the main doorway with arms folded, watching him. Coder met her eyes. She appeared hollow-eyed, yet pale and beautiful. She had always looked beautiful to him.

It was a long moment before she broke the silence. 'And just what are you trying to do, Ryan Coder? Kill yourself?'

'I'm doing fine,' he growled. Then, 'What are you doing up this time of day?'

'I went to your room to see if you were awake.'

'Kind of early for visiting, isn't it?' He frowned. 'Something wrong?'

She drew something from the pocket of her robe and handed it to him wordlessly. The moment Coder unfolded the dodger from Mexico he realized he'd forgotten to go through the Kid's satchels following the gunplay. The dodger announcing the huge reward for killer Kid Silk was vivid and gaudy yet the flashy image was unmistakably of her late brother.

'It's true, isn't it?' she said calmly. 'Danny really was a killer and you lied to us about him?'

He could only shrug. He was very tired now, far

too beat to argue or lie any more.

She drew closer, expression puzzled. 'What I don't understand is, why? Why should you go to such lengths to conceal the truth about my brother?'

'I guess I had my reasons.'

'But only one reason seems to make any kind of sense to me. You lied to save my father pain. So you made out what had happened was all your fault. But it was Danny's, wasn't it? What really happened in the Jimcracks, Ryan Coder?'

'What does it matter now? Look, lady, it's all over, and whether your brother was an outlaw or a travelling preacher don't matter a damn any more.'

'It matters to me, because . . . because what you seem to have done means that you are anything but the cold, heartless man I thought you to be. And now I realize you were also planning to leave behind that money Father promised you.' She shook her head. 'That I simply didn't understand.'

'Don't try,' he said gruffly. 'It's not worth the effort.'

He made to move past but she placed a hand against his chest. 'Where are you going?'

'Mission.'

'And what then?'

Another shrug. 'Back to work.'

'Bounty hunting?' He was lying; that was all over.

'That's my trade.'

'Is that really what you want to do?'

'No,' he said loudly – and had never meant anything more. It had all soured for him. His world and life had all changed and would never be the same again. Yet he attempted a careless smile to show he didn't really give a damn one way or another – and that was just another lie.

'Then you don't have to go back,' she stated firmly. A pause, then, 'You could stay here.'

He blinked. 'Stay here? But—'

'We are deeply in your debt, Mr Coder, my father and I. We'd like the chance to repay that debt. And with Danny dead and my father dying I am going to soon be in desperate need of a strong man here on the Silver Dollar. . . .'

'You're offering me that job?' He was incredulous. Who offered gun-tippers regular work?

'Well, you are plainly a strong man, I was aware of that from the start. What I didn't know then was that you are also a man of compassion . . . and possibly a very lonely one as well.' She smiled for the first time. 'Please say you'll stay, if only for a while?'

Coder shook his head wonderingly. She wanted him to stay!

'I reckon I'd have to think on it some,' he got out at length.

'I'll give you one minute,' she stated, in a return to that bossy way of hers he found so fascinating. Then, as if already assured what his ultimate decision would be, she added, 'I'll have the coffee ready by then. And after that, you are going straight back to bed.'

She was gone.

He stood as though rooted to the spot. It was loco, he told himself. He knew if he stayed on, even for a brief time, he would never want to leave. And he would be six kinds of a fool to believe her invitation meant anything more than what she'd said – that she wanted to repay him a debt. So of course it couldn't possibly work out. . . .

But what if it did?

Wasn't it worth the risk if there was even the slightest hope? He'd faced sudden death more times than he could recall for little more than pride and a fistfull of dollars sometimes. Why would he backwater now with so much more at stake to be won?

Chafing at the delay, the stallion nipped his shoulder. Coder didn't even feel the pain. He turned slowly to see the sun had fully cleared the rim. Then he smiled, walked around the corner and strode swiftly towards the house.

Libby Wardlaw was watching from the kitchen window.